Sharpshooting Señorita

Longarm peeked over the windowsill and watched as Casey and the four gunmen rode into the yard.

When they were within fifteen yards of the prostrate Jed Dodson, Longarm moved away from the window to the door. All five men dismounted and stared at Dodson, who looked dead.

Longarm distinctly heard Casey say, "Roll the old bastard over. I want to see if I got him in the heart."

One of the gunmen stepped over to the body and reached down to turn Jed over onto his back. That's when the old rancher yanked his gun up and shot the gunman squarely in the face.

Longarm saw Casey and the other three men go for their guns, and he jumped out on the front porch and squeezed off both barrels of the shotgun. The thunder was so loud and the recoil so powerful that it knocked him a step back into the doorway. A huge cloud of smoke billowed outward, and then Addie opened fire, her bullets smashing through the front window of Jed's log house . . .

TABOR EVANS

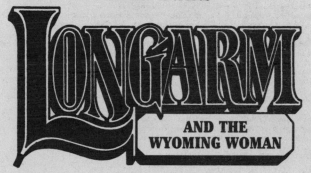

LONGARM

AND THE
WYOMING WOMAN

J

JOVE BOOKS, NEW YORK

THE BERKLEY PUBLISHING GROUP
Published by the Penguin Group
Penguin Group (USA) Inc.
375 Hudson Street, New York, New York 10014, USA
Penguin Group (Canada), 90 Eglinton Avenue East, Suite 700, Toronto, Ontario M4P 2Y3, Canada
(a division of Pearson Penguin Canada Inc.)
Penguin Books Ltd., 80 Strand, London WC2R 0RL, England
Penguin Group Ireland, 25 St. Stephen's Green, Dublin 2, Ireland (a division of Penguin Books Ltd.)
Penguin Group (Australia), 250 Camberwell Road, Camberwell, Victoria 3124, Australia
(a division of Pearson Australia Group Pty. Ltd.)
Penguin Books India Pvt. Ltd., 11 Community Centre, Panchsheel Park, New Delhi—110 017, India
Penguin Group (NZ), 67 Apollo Drive, Rosedale, North Shore 0632, New Zealand
(a division of Pearson New Zealand Ltd.)
Penguin Books (South Africa) (Pty.) Ltd., 24 Sturdee Avenue, Rosebank, Johannesburg 2196,
South Africa

Penguin Books Ltd., Registered Offices: 80 Strand, London WC2R 0RL, England

This is a work of fiction. Names, characters, places, and incidents either are the product of the author's imagination or are used fictitiously, and any resemblance to actual persons, living or dead, business establishments, events, or locales is entirely coincidental.

LONGARM AND THE WYOMING WOMAN

A Jove Book / published by arrangement with the author

PRINTING HISTORY
Jove edition / September 2008

Copyright © 2008 by The Berkley Publishing Group.
Cover illustration by Miro Sinovcic.

ISBN: 978-0-515-14522-9

JOVE®
Jove Books are published by The Berkley Publishing Group,
a division of Penguin Group (USA) Inc.,
375 Hudson Street, New York, New York 10014.
JOVE is a registered trademark of Penguin Group (USA) Inc.
The "J" design is a trademark belonging to Penguin Group (USA) Inc.

PRINTED IN THE UNITED STATES OF AMERICA

10 9 8 7 6 5 4 3 2 1

Chapter 1

Custis Long walked swiftly past the U.S. Mint while bent into a cold November wind that was sweeping off the Front Range of the snowcapped Rocky Mountains. This bitter and blustery Monday morning he was on his way to the Federal Building, where he worked as a deputy United States marshal. As usual, Longarm was running about an hour late. He was impatient as he stopped and waited for an opportunity to sprint across Colfax Avenue, but then he heard a woman screaming for help.

Longarm twisted around in the hard, biting wind and lost his flat-crowned hat, which went sailing up into the sky. Like all of his clothing, the Stetson was expensive, and he would have gone after it had it not been for the shrill cry of distress. His blue-gray eyes swept the morning crowd of workers huddled in heavy clothing as they also looked this way and that to find the source of the trouble. Finally, and just out of the corner of his eye, Longarm saw two large men in wool coats dragging a struggling young woman off the street toward a dark alley.

Longarm was a big man, born and raised in West-by-God-Virginia. Tough and ruthless in a fight, nevertheless

1

he possessed the deeply rooted instincts of a true gentleman of the old school. That meant, no matter what the odds, he would never turn his back on a woman in need.

Longarm wore his double-action Colt revolver on his left hip, and he also carried a hideout twin-barreled .44-caliber derringer that was attached to his watch chain. The derringer wasn't an accurate weapon, but it was deadly at close range. Now, however, he chose the revolver and with gun in hand, he went charging after the two muggers and the girl who had disappeared between a pair of brick buildings.

Longarm was tall and he had the foot speed of a natural athlete, so it only took him a few moments to reach the alley's entrance. He stared down the narrow and dimly lit corridor littered with rubbish, empty whiskey bottles, and dented trash barrels. About fifty yards down the alley where it opened up, he saw that the two brazen muggers had the woman down and were intent on either raping or robbing her on the spot. Maybe they wanted to do both despite the cold wind and weather. The victim's screams were weaker now, and Longarm suspected that the woman had already been knocked half-senseless.

"Freeze, you sonofabitches!" Longarm shouted as he raced forward with his gun in hand.

The muggers glanced up suddenly, and one of them fumbled for a gun on his hip. Longarm skidded to a halt, took a split second to aim, and shot the man through his forehead. He went over backward, heels kicking at the hard dirt and loose garbage.

The second mugger was much wiser. Abandoning his victim, he grabbed her purse and ran for his life.

"Stop him!" the woman cried, pushing herself up on one elbow. "He's stealing all my money!"

2

Longarm hurried up to the young woman, who was trying to climb to her feet but was obviously dazed and in shock. She was very lovely, probably in her mid-twenties, and she wore fashionable clothes that were now ripped and soiled. Her dress and petticoat had been pushed up to her hips, confirming his suspicion that the two would have raped her in the next few minutes. Her legs were long and very white, but he saw that both of her knees were scraped and bleeding. When Longarm reached her, she was struggling to pull her dress and under-garments down to her ankles at the same time that she was frantically attempting to get away from the dead man and his blood, which was forming a dark pool beside her.

"You shot him to death!" It wasn't an accusation, but there was a hint of disbelief in her voice that told Longarm she was unaccustomed to witnessing such sudden and violent death.

"Yes, I shot him before he could shoot me and good riddance." Longarm knelt beside her and helped her cover her bare legs. "Miss, I'm a federal law officer. How bad are you hurt?"

She used her tongue to taste her own bloody lips. In a voice that trembled, she said, "I'll be all right. Please get my purse back!"

Longarm glanced up the alley. The second mugger was escaping. "I'm more concerned about you right now."

"You don't understand! I had just over two thousand dollars in that purse and it's all the money I have in this world."

It was a ridiculous amount of cash for anyone to carry on the street. "Two *thousand* dollars?"

"Yes!" She began to cry. "Those two must have seen

3

me leave the bank and . . . he's getting away! If I lose that money, my father will be ruined!"

"I'll try to catch and arrest him," Longarm said, helping the woman to her feet. "Can you manage to walk back to Colfax? It isn't safe to leave you here alone."

"I can! Now go after him! Please!"

Because the woman sounded so desperate and the amount of her loss was so large, Longarm took off after the second mugger. He had no doubt that he could outrun the man despite his big head start. Longarm was concerned that, if the mugger ducked back onto Colfax or one of the other streets, he would quickly mingle with the morning crowd on its way to work in downtown Denver. Once that happened, the odds were that he would make good his escape and be two thousand dollars richer.

The mugger, probably thinking that there was not going to be a pursuit, paused to catch his breath about a hundred yards ahead at the exit from the alley. He was bent over gasping for air, and Longarm could tell that he was badly winded and in poor physical condition despite his size. Longarm didn't say a word as he ran forward as silently as possible in the hope that the mugger wouldn't look back until it was too late to escape.

But the mugger *did* look back, and when he saw the broad-shouldered federal officer coming at him with a gun in his fist, the man whirled and disappeared. Longarm rounded the corner exiting the alley back on to Colfax just in time to see the mugger knock over a couple of pedestrians and then vanish into the morning crowd.

"Hey, stop!" Longarm shouted, knowing that the man wasn't about to stop. A moment later, Longarm got

4

lucky when he saw the mugger try to cross the busy downtown street and then get struck by a buggy. The mugger was knocked down, but got up and started limping toward a nearby park in the direction of Cherry Creek. Longarm knew that that was a place where many of the worst dregs in Denver tended to congregate.

"Stop," Longarm ordered again as he swiftly overtook the mugger. "Stop or I'll shoot!"

The mugger was limping badly and had run as far as he was able. Realizing he was about to be overtaken, he stopped and twisted around. He shouted a curse that was lost in the wind, and then he grabbed an old woman and used her as a shield, holding his gun to her head.

For a moment, everything froze in time. Longarm skidded to a halt, and the most striking thing he noticed was the old woman's eyes, which were filled with terror.

"You go away or I'll blow her damned brains out!" the mugger cried at Longarm. "I mean it! Turn and get away from here now!"

Longarm studied the man's face. It was dirty, scarred, and twisted with anger rather than raw fear or panic. This, Longarm knew from past experience, was a man that had nothing to lose.

"All right," Longarm said, lowering his Colt revolver until it rested by his leg. "Just take it easy, mister. There's no point in getting anyone else killed. Not over a stolen purse."

"You shot my friend back there in that alley!"

"We both know that I had no choice . . . it was self-defense," Longarm said, trying to figure out how he was going to defuse this situation enough to save the old woman and yet still gain the upper hand.

"Are you a lawman?"

"Yes. I'm a federal officer. Drop the gun and you'll only go to jail for a while."

But instead of surrendering, the mugger cursed and cocked his pistol. The old woman was frightened and she fainted dead away. The mugger had her in a throat lock and the barrel of his gun was pressed tightly to her skull as he shouted, "I ain't goin' back to jail or any prison. Never again! You got just two choices, turn around and go away . . . or watch me blow out this old lady's brains."

"You win," Longarm said, realizing that this man would do exactly what he had threatened. "I'm going away, but first let go of that woman."

"Move!" the mugger shouted.

Longarm turned and walked off expecting a bullet in the back. His heart was pounding when he rounded a street corner, and then immediately turned and pressed himself to the building to see if the mugger was going to do as he'd promised.

The mugger dropped the unconscious woman to the sidewalk, then with his gun still raised in case anyone else planned to interfere, he looked frantically around and started backing in between two buildings. Longarm could see that the man was going to return to the same alley that they'd exited only a few minutes earlier, so he ducked his head and sprinted down the dark corridor between a nearby set of buildings.

A cat that he almost trampled screeched, rats scuttled through piles of garbage, but Longarm was too focused to notice until he came back to the alley. He bent over for a moment to catch his breath, then heard the pounding of running feet and smiled with cold satisfaction. The mugger was coming closer, not moving farther away.

Gun up and with five beans still in the can, Longarm stepped out and the mugger almost collided with him. The light was poor, the air was cold, and the early winter wind was cutting through the corridors of brick and stone and making an eerie, shrieking sound. The mugger cried out in surprise, then tried to reverse direction and run away, but he slipped and fell. Rolling hard with a painful grunt, he turned and tried to get his pistol up and shoot.

Longarm figured that he'd given the fellow enough chances to live another day. The distance being close, he didn't need to aim as he shot the mugger twice in the chest. The man cried out, and then fell back on the dirty alley floor still trying to pull off a shot.

Kicking the gun from the dying man's fist, Longarm held his fire and watched the mugger gasp his last few breaths as the front of his dirty woolen coat began soaking up a large quantity of fresh blood.

"What's your name, mister?" Longarm asked, kneeling beside the dying mugger. "You don't deserve it, but if you have family, I'll do my best to see that they know you're gone."

The mugger stared up at Longarm, rolling his head back and forth. With bloody froth on his lips, he hissed, "I'll see you in hell!"

"Could be, but you'll be there for damned certain."

The man tried to spit on Longarm, but instead coughed up blood and then went still.

Longarm collected the young woman's stolen purse and the mugger's pistol. It only took a moment to search the mugger's pockets and, as he'd expected, he found no identification.

Just before leaving the body, Longarm studied the

man a moment and said, "Somewhere, you have family . . . and maybe they're even good, churchgoing people who have always loved and forgiven you. . .but I expect that you'd just as soon not have them know that you died in this filthy alley after attempting rape and robbery."

Longarm reloaded his gun. "Don't worry. Whatever family you and that other sonofabitch came from will never know how you met your sad and well-deserved end."

And with that, Longarm turned and headed up the alley back toward Colfax Avenue. He would find the beautiful young woman and return her purse and money. Then he would go on to the office and his boss would wonder why he was especially late this cold, bitter Monday morning. Marshal Billy Vail would just naturally assume that Longarm had been delayed by a woman. A young and beautiful woman who would want one more vigorous bout of lovemaking before sending Custis off to work.

Well, Longarm thought as he holstered his six-gun, *this is one Monday morning that Billy will at least be half right.*

Chapter 2

"You got my purse back!" the young woman cried, running forward and then snatching the purse from Longarm a moment before she gave him a kiss and a hug despite the pain her split lip must have caused her. "You're my hero!"

Despite the cold wind, a crowd was gathered around the girl, and now they smiled and some even applauded. Longarm was a modest man, and he blushed and tried to make light of his accomplishment. "It wasn't really a problem," he said to the woman. "Neither one of those muggers could shoot straight."

She looked up at him with one eye already swollen shut. "Did you have to kill them *both*?"

"I'm afraid that I did," Longarm admitted. "Miss, I'll take you to the nearest police station because they'll want to ask you a few questions and take a statement about the robbery and my gunfight."

"Do you know who those two thieves were?"

"No. And it's very possible we may never learn their true identities. Those types aren't likely to carry identification. They could be drifters."

She opened her purse and peered inside. Longarm followed her glance, and he saw a thick roll of greenbacks.

"I'm sure it's all here," the woman said with a huge sigh of relief. "Every last dollar."

"They darned sure didn't have a chance to spend any of it," Longarm answered.

"No, they didn't."

Longarm held out his arm. "Miss, can I escort you to the police station?"

"Thank you."

A well-dressed stranger came up to Longarm and handed him his Stetson. "I saw it blow off your head and then sail into the sky for a few minutes before coming back down on the street. I thought it was the least I could do for someone as brave as you, Marshal."

Longarm thanked the man and reset his hat firmly. "Does anyone know what happened to the older woman that the mugger tried to use as a shield until she fainted?" he asked, looking up the street.

"She recovered and then was helped off to see a doctor," someone told Longarm. "Needless to say, she was very upset."

"I'm just glad she wasn't hurt."

"Marshal," a woman told him. "I hope you receive a commendation from the city for your bravery."

"Thanks, but that's not too likely," Longarm told her, not a bit interested in a commendation. "I was just doing my job."

He turned to the woman who'd been assaulted and robbed. "Miss, if you're ready, I'll escort you to the police station. It's only two blocks away, if you feel up to it. If not, we'll find a cab driver and—"

"No," she said. "My knees are scraped up, but I'm more than grateful for your kindness and the way this turned out. I just wish that those two men hadn't been shot to death."

"It was their own choice," Longarm told her. "I gave both of 'em every chance to surrender. They were mean and ruthless, miss. You shouldn't waste much time mourning their loss."

"I suppose not," she agreed, forcing a smile that caused her to wince with pain. "I do know you're right and they've probably hurt many others besides myself and that dear old woman."

"Bet on it," Longarm reassured her.

"My name is Adeline Hudson. *Miss* Adeline Hudson. But you certainly have bravely earned the right to just call me Addie."

"Custis Long," he said, bowing slightly. "The pleasure is mine."

"No," she said sweetly, "the pleasure is most certainly all mine."

It was amazing, Longarm thought, how a beautiful young woman who had only moments earlier nearly been strangled and raped could now appear so joyful and unaffected.

"Have you had breakfast yet, Marshal?"

Longarm shook his head. "No."

"Then let me buy you a nice breakfast. It's the least that I can do to show my appreciation."

"We should report in to the local police station first," he told her. "After all, there are two bodies to be recovered by the undertaker and paperwork to fill out. All that takes time, I'm afraid."

She looked up at him. "I imagine you know from similar past experiences."

Longarm nodded, not in the least bit proud of all the men he had killed despite the fact that every last one of the late sonofabitches had earned a well-deserved and swift journey to the nearest cemetery. "I'm afraid you're correct," he admitted.

Addie suddenly faltered.

"Are you all right?" Longarm asked with concern.

"I suddenly feel rather faint," she told him.

"Maybe we should get you to a doctor."

"No," Addie said. "It's just delayed shock plus the fact that I haven't had anything yet to eat today. I think hunger and the shock are just now catching up with me."

They were standing outside a café that Longarm often frequented and that he knew was very good. "Then let's go inside and have something to eat," he decided. "We can't have you fainting and banging up those pretty knees again, now can we?"

She took a deep breath and managed a radiant smile. "So you thought my knees were pretty?"

He blushed slightly. "Well, I couldn't help but notice they were very pretty. As were your legs."

Now it was Addie's turn to blush. "Modesty forbids a response," she told him. "But I have to say that I'm glad you thought my legs were attractive."

He helped her inside. "I have a habit of speaking exactly what is on my mind, Addie."

"That's good," she replied, sliding into a booth. "So do I. And that's why I have to admit that I'm very attracted to you, Marshal. You have no idea how much it means to me that you recovered all that money. I must think of some way to repay you."

12

"Not necessary," he assured her as he slid into the booth next to her.

"Oh, but it *is* necessary! You see, that money I almost lost is for my father, who owns a ranch near a town called Buffalo Falls, Wyoming. He's desperately trying to save our land from being taken over by a very powerful and unscrupulous man who wants to have him evicted. The two thousand dollars will be used to hire good lawyers to defend my father's claim."

"Then I'm glad that I was able to save it for you," Longarm told her.

"My father will want to thank you personally."

"That's not necessary."

"Maybe sometime you could come to see our ranch. It's very scenic and—"

"They keep me pretty busy," Longarm told her. "Sometimes, I get sent out on assignments on a day's notice."

"Well, today is almost half over, so I doubt you'll be leaving before tomorrow."

"I expect not."

"I'd like to see you for dinner at my place . . . my treat."

Longarm was interested. By rights, he should have insisted that dinner certainly wasn't necessary. But something told him that more was being offered than a good meal . . . much, much more.

So he merely smiled with appreciation and said, "I'd like that, Addie."

She reached across the table and squeezed his hand. "You are really something special, Custis. And I want to know all about you."

"Not much to tell."

"I don't believe that for a minute."

They ordered breakfast, and Longarm and Addie lost track of time. When they finally left the restaurant, it was almost noon. That being the case, Longarm decided that he might as well spend the lunch hour with Addie after they reported in to the local police.

His boss would be furious, but when Billy Vail learned that Longarm had saved the lives of two women and rid the city of a pair of vicious muggers and thieves, he would be more than forgiving.

Chapter 3

"Custis!"

Longarm waved and strolled between the desks at his office. He could see his boss, Billy Vail, gesturing wildly for him to come right in at once. But Longarm didn't hurry, and his coworkers were grinning because he was defiantly their outlaw, the maverick of the office. They knew that he could get away with plenty because he was indispensable. Still, coming in on Monday in the middle of the afternoon with lipstick smeared on his cheek was sure to create quite a row with the boss.

"Where the hell have you been all morning!" Billy shouted. "Close that door."

Longarm turned to see the office staff watching in anticipation. "Sorry, folks," he said, closing the door to Billy's private office.

He could see the disappointment on their faces, but there was no help for it, so he turned around, grinned, and said, "Hello there, Billy! I hope your week is off to a good start."

It was a deliberate jab meant to get a strong reaction from his boss, and it worked. "A good start! Dammit,

15

Custis, who do you think you are, King Solomon? Everyone else who works in this building—and there must be a hundred or more—seems capable of arriving to work on time. But not you! No, not the great Longarm! Can't you understand that you set a terrible example, especially for the newer people? How am I expected to have any discipline in this office if I allow you to come and go whenever you feel like it!"

Longarm pulled a cheroot out of his vest pocket and took a seat. "Want a smoke?" he offered with a smile.

"Hell, no! You smoke *dog turds*!"

"Wrong," Longarm said, still smiling as he scratched a match on the bottom of his boot and lit up. "These are absolutely Mexico's finest."

"Dog turds!" Billy reached into a humidor and produced a long, handsome Cuban cigar. "Now *these* are real cigars. And they don't smell like burning shit!"

"Ah, you're right," Longarm said in pleasant agreement. "But you make so much more of a salary than I do that I just can't afford the best, Billy. When you're a poor, overworked deputy marshal, you have to drink and smoke what you can afford."

"Oh, horseshit!"

Longarm raised his eyebrows in question. "Dogshit? Horseshit? Billy, you seem to be sorta fixated on shit today. What's the matter? Trouble at home? Want to talk about it man-to-man?"

Billy got red in the face and pounded his fine mahogany desk. "Don't you bait me today, Custis. I'm in no mood for it."

Longarm blew a smoke ring at the ceiling and studied Billy, trying to figure out why he was so much on the prod today. It had to be more than the fact that Longarm was a few hours late to the office. Longarm knew that this man had once been a lowly field man like himself and he'd been good at his job, earning many commendations for bravery. But then Billy had gotten married, sired a passel of kids, and taken office promotions until now . . . now he was just another well-paid bureaucrat, a pudgy pencil pusher. But Marshal Billy Vail was still a fine, intelligent man, and Longarm figured it was time to get serious and show his boss a little badly needed respect.

"Billy," he said, "I apologize for not coming in like everyone else this morning. I had fully intended to be on time, but I got into a fix when two muggers tried to rob a woman less than a block from our office. I had no choice but to step in and straighten things out."

"Did you arrest 'em?"

"No. I killed 'em."

Billy's jaw dropped. "Jaysus! You already *killed* two men this morning?"

"Yeah, I'm afraid so. But I swear that they had it coming. They actually assaulted two women. One of them was a sweet old lady that was so upset she was rushed to a doctor. So you see, Boss, I was working this morning to rid the city of two very dangerous criminals."

Billy Vail never quite knew when Longarm was pulling his leg. His best deputy could do that with a straight face and you just didn't know if he was serious or on the level. With any of his other officers, the story that Billy had just heard would seem preposterous . . . but not with Longarm. With Longarm, damn near anything was possible.

"Give me the full story and don't leave out any details," Billy ordered, leaning back in his office chair and puffing on his Cuban cigar.

Longarm told it straight, and ended up saying, "I took the young woman to the local police station and we gave sworn testimony to what happened and I wrote out their official report. The captain sent one of his men to the alley and they identified both of the bodies. Those men had mugged several other innocent women before and were wanted criminals. The captain thanked me over and over for saving him and his department the trouble of finding, arresting, and then sending them to court and prison."

Billy was fiddling with a pencil. "Oh he did, did he?"

"Yep," Longarm said. "Said I saved the taxpayers a lot of grief and money. Said he'd hire me in a minute if you decided to fire me for being so late to the office today."

"Don't try to be funny," Billy warned. "I'm not in the mood for your poor jokes today."

"Billy, what's really wrong? You're more out of sorts than I've seen you in a long time."

Billy sighed and leaned forward across his cluttered desk. "I'm sure you remember Wade Stoneman."

Longarm scowled at the mention of that name. "Of course. We even worked a few cases together shortly after I came here."

"Then you know that Wade Stoneman left this department under a bad cloud. Some of the federal prosecutors were livid when he was relieved of his duties and allowed to go without being arrested."

Longarm remembered that being the case. "Stoneman was accused of murdering a witness and taking money for hire."

"That's right. However, as I'm sure you are aware, the witness that would have sent Stoneman to either prison or the gallows was murdered and his killer was never found. Everyone was sure that Stoneman killed the man, but we couldn't get any evidence. People were scared to death of the man and nobody was talking. The result was that Wade Stoneman left Denver a free man. Some of us were relieved but torn with doubt because he'd been a fine federal marshal for a number of years. I don't have to tell you that he was the best man I had and he never failed me no matter how dangerous the case he was assigned. He was the best we had in this agency."

Longarm's eyes narrowed. "The best before I joined up."

"That's right," Billy said. "Wade was smart, tough, and brave. Fearless actually. He lived hard and on the edge . . . somewhat like you live, Custis."

"That's not quite true."

"Be it true or not, Wade was a department legend. Wherever I sent him, he did the job and very rarely did he take prisoners."

"He was a stone-cold killer," Longarm said flatly. "He just had a federal officer's badge to hide behind all the blood he spilled."

Billy leaned back in his chair. "Is that what you *really* thought of the man?"

"Yep. It was and still is." Longarm's mood darkened at the memory of Stoneman. "I saw Wade shoot down two ragged kids not yet out of their teens who had stolen a sorry old saddle that couldn't have been worth more than two or three dollars."

"You did?"

"That's right. It was in Cheyenne on a November day

about as raw as this one. The kids were poor and stole the saddle intending to sell it for food or maybe firewood. Stoneman tracked them down that day and shot them without giving them the chance to go to jail. I doubt they'd even have spent a day in the local jail. But instead of a jail, they wound up in a damned cemetery."

"Why didn't you stop him?" Billy asked, his voice reflecting shock and no small measure of bitterness.

"I wasn't there when the shooting happened. I'm sure that Wade knew I wouldn't allow him to kill those two boys, so he slipped out on me and cornered those young fellas, then gunned them down."

"Sonofabitch!"

"Yeah, that's what he is," Longarm said. "I heard him whistling 'Dixie' that night just as happy as a songbird. Wade Stoneman had no conscience. He was one of the most ruthless men I've ever known, and also one of the best with a gun or a rifle. For that matter, he was quite a knife fighter, too."

Billy shook his head and studied the tip of his cigar. "How come you never told me about those boys that Wade gunned down?"

"What was the point?"

"Maybe we could have investigated and . . ."

"Bullshit!" Longarm swore. "Those boys were dead and I was new on the job. Back then, you thought Wade Stoneman was the second coming of Jesus Christ. He walked on water, Billy. Besides, I wasn't there to see the shooting, so I had to rely on an old man who saw it and was so scared of Marshal Stoneman that he told me what happened and then immediately left Cheyenne on the fastest horse he could buy. So, without proof of the murders, what could I do against a highly touted fellow law officer?"

"I see your point," Billy admitted.

"Let's get back to the present," Longarm suggested. "What has Wade Stoneman done now and why are we even talking about him?"

"He's completely gone over to the darkness," Billy said. "He became a local marshal in Wyoming."

"And?"

Billy picked up a telegram. "I got this as soon as I came to work this morning. It says that Wade Stoneman has recently gunned down four prominent men, three city councilmen and the mayor. Stoneman is now not only the new mayor, but owner of the local bank and a growing land company. People there are begging us, or anyone who will investigate, to stop him before he kills more innocent people in his quest for money and power."

"Sounds like ex-Federal Marshal Wade Stoneman has gotten real ambitious since he left our office."

"Yeah, it does." Billy tried to blow a smoke ring to equal Longarm's, but he failed. "A man that cunning, deadly, and probably now quite wealthy adds up to being a very formidable enemy."

Longarm nodded in agreement. "Billy, are you thinking of sending *me* over there?"

"It has crossed my mind a time or two this morning."

Longarm puffed faster. "I'd just as soon you didn't."

"Why?"

"It sounds like a no-win situation. Wade Stoneman and I didn't part as friends . . . quite the opposite. Furthermore, he'll immediately recognize me as someone you sent, and there goes any chance I might have to snoop around and try to get some evidence against him. And finally, I really don't want to have to brace the man."

Billy nodded. "Because he's faster than you?"

"Maybe."

Billy sighed. "Then forget it, Custis. I'll send someone else."

"Why send anyone?" Longarm asked. "This isn't a federal case. It's a case for the local sheriff to handle."

"He died rather suddenly of lead poisoning."

"No witnesses?" Longarm asked, already knowing the answer.

"None at all."

Longarm sat in silence and smoked for a few minutes, remembering Wade Stoneman and those two young kids who had foolishly stolen an old saddle to get some food money for themselves and maybe their families. Those boys were resting in a cemetery, and by now their simple wooden grave markers would have rotted and fallen over as casualties of Wyoming's hard wind, rain, and snow. Most likely, no one remembered them or laid flowers on their graves. Nope, they'd died young and poor.

And, gawdammit, entirely unnecessarily.

"I'll go," Longarm said, making his decision.

"I've decided that you shouldn't."

"I said I'll go!"

Billy stared at Longarm across from his desk. "You just put your finger on it when you said that Wade Stoneman probably hasn't committed any federal crimes. So you'll have no jurisdiction and no justification for going after the man."

"I'll think of something," Longarm replied.

"If what I've learned in this telegram is the truth, you're going to be up against more than you've ever had to handle before."

"I enjoy real challenges."

Billy nodded. "When can you leave for Wyoming?"

Thinking of Addie, he said, "I have special plans for tonight. However, I can catch the Union Pacific tomorrow and be in Cheyenne by nightfall. From there, either rent a horse or take a stagecoach. What's the name of the town that Wade Stoneman has in his grip?"

"You've probably never heard of it. I haven't. It's called . . ." Billy glanced down at the telegram. "It's called Buffalo Falls."

Longarm almost dropped his cigar on the desk. "Buffalo Falls?"

"Yes, have you heard of it?"

Longarm dipped his chin. "As a matter of fact, I just heard of it this morning."

"Really?"

"Yes," Longarm replied. "And maybe I even know the name of the man who sent the telegram."

"It's unsigned. I'm sure that whoever sent this was afraid of being found out and killed by Stoneman."

"Wouldn't surprise me a bit," Longarm said, coming out of his chair. "Billy?"

"Yeah?"

"Can you meet me tomorrow at the train station with my traveling money?"

"Yes. I'll have it ready."

"Don't send me there on the cheap," Longarm warned. "I'll need the best horse and outfit I can buy in Cheyenne."

"You'll have it. Just don't let Wade Stoneman make you another notch on the butt of his gun."

"I'll try not to," Longarm said, heading out of the office without even a trace of his earlier smile.

Chapter 4

They skipped the pot roast that Addie had prepared. Skipped the fresh apple pie, too. Instead, the moment that Longarm walked into her apartment, they embraced and began kissing each other passionately.

"Where's your bedroom?" he whispered.

"You're not hungry?"

Custis laughed and began to unbutton her dress. "I'm hungry, all right. But my hunger for you far outweighs the hunger in my belly."

"But I thought we'd have a nice dinner with wine and . . ." Addie nearly swooned. "Take it easy on my lips," she pleaded. "The lower one is split."

"And you've got quite the shiner," Longarm said, "but I'm not interested in your lips and eyes as much as I'm interested in what's under this dress."

She pretended to pout. "You're an animal!"

"I guess I am," he agreed, getting frustrated with the buttons and tearing her dress off, then yanking down her petticoat and underwear.

"Oh," she moaned, "I think I'm going to be assaulted for the second time today."

"Yeah, you are," he agreed, his hand slipping between her legs to find her honey pot already wet. "But I promise that you'll like it this time."

Addie was nearly breathless. "Come on," she pleaded, dragging him toward a small bedroom. "You've got me so excited I'm already about to go crazy."

"It'll get worse," he said, pushing her down on the bed and unbuckling his gunbelt, then kicking off his boots.

She tried to get up, but he leaned forward and pushed her back down on the pink bedspread. "Please," she whispered, "this bedspread is brand-new and expensive. At least let me turn it back so that we don't get it spotted and stained."

"Okay," he said, finishing undressing, "but what I'm going to give you isn't going to be wasted on the bedspread. You're getting it *all*, Addie. Every drop."

Addie giggled and pulled the bedspread aside. She tore off the last of her clothes and jumped on the bed spreading her long legs. "Come and get me, big boy!"

Longarm wasn't a man who believed in a whole lot of foreplay, at least not the first time he took a woman. So he grabbed his big tool and aimed it right where it wanted to go, and then he rammed it into Addie's honey pot all the way.

"Oh, my gosh!" she cried. "I feel like I've just been mounted by a wild stallion."

"Then pretend that you're a frisky young filly," he grunted, slamming his rod in and out and then bending down and licking her taut nipples until they stood up like fresh strawberries.

Addie was no virgin, but it was clear that she wasn't

as experienced as Longarm in the art of lovemaking. Longarm felt her wrap her long legs around his hips, and he purposely slowed his thrusting. With all the self-control he could muster, he began to rotate his hips, making sure that his rod was stroking her sweet little rosebud. In less than two minutes, Addie started humping and moaning, and it was clear that she was getting ready for an eruption of epic proportions.

"Oh, dear heavens, Custis, you're amazing. I can't believe that I'm already going to come and you're just getting started. It's never happened to me so quick as—oh, oh!"

Addie went wild under Longarm, screeching and scratching and wailing with ecstasy. Longarm grinned and bore down on her even harder until he felt like a volcano was erupting between his legs, and then he was driving his hot seed deep into Addie while she threw her head back and forth and howled like a wildcat.

"Oh, don't stop," she whispered a few moments later. "Don't ever stop."

"I'm finished for the moment," he said, damned pleased for giving her every bit as much pleasure as he'd enjoyed.

"Just stir me a couple minutes longer," she pleaded. "It still feels so . . . so gawdamn good!"

Longarm was more than happy to oblige. But after a while, he could feel his root starting to soften, and so he rolled off Addie.

"You devastated me, Custis. You devastated and ravished me!"

"If you want, I'll do it again after we eat," he promised.

"I'll do it over and over tonight until you are so satisfied you won't know if you should laugh . . . or cry."

She ran her fingers over her flat belly and then down to the place where he'd just planted his seed. "It feels like it's on fire, but a sweet fire. Custis, in all honesty, I don't know how much of you I can take."

"We'll have fun finding out," he said. "And when you can't take anymore, I promise you I'll stop."

She began to giggle. "You are the best I ever had, Marshal. And I mean that sincerely."

"You're pretty special yourself," he said. "When do we eat?"

She sat up, and then was a little wobbly getting to her feet. "I'm going to leak all over the place. I need a few minutes alone."

"Sure." Longarm grabbed his pants and left the bedroom, fully understanding the lady's urgent need for privacy. He went back into the living room and found a bottle of wine, which he opened. Two crystal wineglasses were soon filled and as he sipped one glass empty, he studied the room and its furnishings.

There were a number of daguerreotypes and photographs, sepia-toned and showing Addie Hudson with her parents. In one picture, they were standing on the porch of a nice ranch house; in another, the parents stood by a hitching rail and Addie, about fifteen years old, was astride a pinto pony. Longarm studied the faces of Addie's parents, and he could see a strong resemblance between the girl and her mother. The father looked like an old-time cowboy with an impressive white handlebar mustache that drooped at the tips. His white hair was parted exactly down the middle, while a big pair of workingman's hands held a battered black Stetson. Addie's father was tall and slightly bowlegged. The mother was prim and proper, but Longarm could see a lot of strength in her face and in the way her chin was proudly raised for the family photographs.

There were no other children that Longarm could see, so he supposed that Addie just might be an only child. That was unusual on the frontier, where large families were more common.

The furniture in Addie's living room was nice, but nothing special. Longarm was surprised to see a saddle in the corner, and it had obviously been made for a woman or child because the seat was small. The saddle had silver conchos and it was beautifully made. Stamped in the back of the cantle was a single word, ADDIE.

"Did you find anything interesting?" Addie asked, exiting her bedroom in a stunning lacy nightgown that immediately rekindled Longarm's desire.

"I was just admiring the daguerreotypes and photographs of you and your family."

"My mother passed away long ago and I still miss her terribly, but not as bad as Father does. He doesn't look much different today than he did back then. He's still ramrod-straight and strong."

"I'm sorry to hear about your mother's passing."

Addie nodded and swallowed hard. "She died in childbirth. The doctor said she was too old and not strong enough to have a second child, but she very much wanted to give my father a son so she just . . . well, she took her chances and it didn't work out."

Longarm could see that Addie was near tears. "In

some of these pictures you look like a little cowboy," he said. "Did you sort of double for a son?"

She sniffled and brightened. "As a matter of fact I did! At a very early age, I learned how to ride and rope. And I'm really a pretty good hand with horses and cattle. I can even shoot straight."

In a playful gesture, Addie raised both hands, index finger pointed to the ceiling, and pretended to shoot a pair of pistols.

Longarm chuckled. "Riding, roping, and shooting are good things to know how to do . . . even for a girl."

"I'm no longer a girl," she said, coming over to give him a kiss. "I'm a woman."

"Yeah," he said, running a hand up and under the nightgown to caress her firm buttocks. "That's for sure."

They began kissing, and Longarm felt his manhood rising to the occasion, but Addie finally pushed him back and panted, "We've got to eat. If you're going to ravish me over and over, I might die if I don't get some food."

"Then let's eat that pot roast," he said, going into the little kitchen and refilling his own wineglass while bringing Addie the other. He raised his glass in a toast. "To us!"

"To us," she said, eyes shining with happiness. "You know, I can't believe that you saved me and my money only this morning. Maybe it sounds silly, but it really seems as if I've known you before. It was such an . . . an amazing coincidence that we happened to come together on Colfax Avenue just the way that we did this morning. And now look at us!"

"We didn't waste any time," he said. Longarm glanced

down at the erection pushing his pants out embarrassingly far, and then felt his cheeks warm. "And look at me down there!"

Addie slipped her hand into his pants and gave him a firm squeeze. When he started to put his wine down and grab her, she backed away saying, "Oh, no, you don't! We'll get back to the bedroom after we eat, big boy! I promise you'll love my pot roast and the dessert I've baked."

"You're my dessert."

"Oh, you don't want any fresh apple pie?" she asked, raising her eyebrows questioningly.

Longarm loved apple pie. "Well, yes, I do. I'll take a big slice of that pie and then I'll take a big poke into *your* little pie. How's that?"

They both started laughing. "Sit down at the table while I start getting food on the table."

"Yes, ma'am."

They chatted about lots of things over dinner, and it was only when they were finished with the apple pie that Longarm said, "Addie, I need to talk to you about tomorrow."

"Why even think about tomorrow when we still have all of tonight?"

"I would really like to know why you were carrying so much cash this morning?"

Her smile faded. "I know that wasn't smart. But I had sold some family things and borrowed a little money from a rich lady friend. I was on my way to the train depot to buy a one-way ticket to Cheyenne."

Longarm could guess the reason. "You were going home to help your father in Buffalo Falls."

"Yes, I was. I mean, I *am*. I have to, Custis. And I'm so sorry, because I don't want to leave you now that we've just found each other, but my father's life and everything he loves is in danger of being lost!"

"Tell me more about what is going so badly for your father in Buffalo Falls."

"I don't know a lot about it," she admitted. "My father sent me away to stay here in Denver while I learned doctoring."

"Doctoring?"

"That's right. Did you know that Denver has one of the few university-trained women doctors in the entire West?"

"I believe I did read something about her in the newspaper a while back," he replied.

"Her name is Dr. Grace Huntington and she studied in England. No medical school would accept her in America, so she and other women have been forced to go to Europe where they are a little more progressive. My father wanted me to go to a medical school in Europe, but I just couldn't bear to leave him for so long, and the expense really made the whole idea out of the question. So he and I compromised, and I wrote to Dr. Huntington three years ago about becoming her assistant with the idea of learning and practicing medicine when I returned to Buffalo Falls, Wyoming."

"And she agreed."

"Not at first. But I'm persistent and I kept writing Grace . . . I mean Dr. Huntington. Finally, I just came and camped out on her office doorstep until she gave in and agreed to teach me medicine."

"So you're a doctor?"

She shrugged. "Not really. I mean, I don't have university training and I couldn't practice surgery in a big-city hospital."

"I was in the Civil War," Longarm said, not wanting to think about that horror of blood and death. "I saw plenty of surgeons and most of them were no better than livestock butchers. Their amputations were crude and the soldiers often bled to death screaming in agony."

"I know," Addie said. "And while I was never at a battlefield like you must have been, I have heard that the battlefield casualties during the War Between the States were overwhelming. But in defense of those army doctors, you have to understand that a battlefield surgeon would have had no time to spare tying off all the blood vessels after amputation because there were so many other wounded soldiers bleeding to death at the same time."

"Let's talk about something else," Longarm said. "I want to talk about you and Buffalo Falls."

"There's no doctor near that town for over a hundred miles," she said. "Being a woman, people won't accept me as a healer at first. But when I start delivering babies, fixing broken bones, suturing up terrible wounds, and saving lives and limbs, they'll come around. I know that for a fact."

Longarm shook his head with amazement. "You're quite a woman, Addie. I can't believe I was lucky enough to meet you."

"I'm the one that was lucky," she said. "You saved me and the money. Money that my father desperately needs to hire attorneys, and maybe even someone who is good with a gun."

"Who is he up against?"

"A terrible, ruthless, and cold-blooded killer named Wade Stoneman," Addie said, her voice taking on a hard edge. "I've never met him, but Father says he is taking over Buffalo Falls and every ranch that he can lay his bloody hands on through any lawless means necessary. Have you ever heard of the man?"

Longarm drained his wineglass and refilled it. "I'm afraid so. I have not only heard of Wade Stoneman, but I once worked with him."

Addie's wineglass slipped from her hand and shattered on the floor. But she didn't bend to clean it up; she just stared at Longarm. "Custis, you can't be serious!"

"I'm afraid that I am."

Longarm bent to pick up pieces of glass and to help Addie clean up the mess, but she grabbed him and said, "Are you . . . are you a friend of his?"

"No!" He lowered his voice. "Wade Stoneman was a deputy United States marshal when I first came to work as a new federal law officer. I was assigned to learn under Wade because he was the best. But then he crossed the boundaries of the law again and again, so that I could see that the man was without a conscience. After he killed a few people without even attempting to arrest them, I asked to be assigned to some other senior federal agent. Wade never forgave me for that and swore that he'd been betrayed. He had thought of me almost as a younger brother. He taught me things that have saved my life. But I never wanted to be like him and I never have been."

Longarm decided that Addie had had enough troubles today and it would do her no good to learn about the two boys that Wade Stoneman had gunned down for stealing an old, broken saddle.

"Here," he said, finding another wineglass and refilling it for her. "We can talk about Stoneman later and I'll tell you more if you want . . . but I'm not sure you want to hear stories about how ruthless and cunning that man can be."

"He's the one that is after my father."

"Addie, let's sit down for a minute. I have something to tell you. Something important."

Longarm led the young woman over to the couch, and then he sat down next to her and thought a moment before he said, "After I left you this afternoon, I went to my office and was told by my boss that I need to go to Buffalo Falls and investigate Wade Stoneman."

"Are you serious?"

"I'm afraid so. A telegram came to my boss's office begging for help. There was no signature, but maybe it was from your father."

"It wasn't," Addie said with certainty. "My father never begged for help from anyone. The telegram had to come from someone else in Buffalo Falls."

"It doesn't matter. The point is that I'm going there and I'll be leaving on the train tomorrow."

"Then I'll leave with you!"

"I'd rather you waited a week or two," Longarm told her.

"But why!"

"You'd be a distraction for me. I'd be thinking of you and worrying about Stoneman and what he might do to both you and your father."

Addie set her glass down, and then she set his glass down on the table and looked into his eyes. "Custis," she said, "I am overwhelmed by you and the way that you just made love to me."

"Addie, that—"

"Please! Let me finish. But I can't stay here in Denver while you go to Buffalo Falls. And don't you see that the coincidence of you saving my life and our family's money . . . and then learning that you're being sent to Buffalo Falls . . . is an omen?"

He didn't get it. "Omen?"

"Okay, maybe not an omen," she persisted. "But it's a clear sign. A sign that we were meant to go to Buffalo Falls together and fight this terrible man until he is either dead or in prison!"

"Addie," Longarm said, "I fear no man, but Wade Stoneman is . . . is, well, he's the best at killing that I've ever seen. He is an absolute crack shot with rifle or pistol and he's inhumanly quick on the draw. You add that to the fact that Wade Stoneman is now wealthy and will have killers in his employ, and it all adds up to long odds against beating him."

"All the more reason I have to come with you!"

"I wish you'd give me a week or two head start."

"And stay here wondering if you and my father were killed by Stoneman?" She shook her head emphatically. "Not a chance. If we lose this fight, I want to lose it together. I just couldn't live with myself if I was here safe while you and Father were up against such impossible odds. Can't you, of all people, understand that?"

Addie was nearly begging, and Longarm could see that she was right. Had he been in her position, he would have taken exactly the same stance. Absolutely nothing could have kept him safe in Denver waiting for the outcome of a showdown taking place in Wyoming.

"All right," he said, "we'll go together. We'll leave on the train for Cheyenne tomorrow."

Addie hugged his neck so hard, he thought she might crack bones. And she cried. Longarm couldn't stand women crying, but in this case it all seemed entirely understandable.

Addie pushed back from him and wiped her eyes. "Custis, we're not going to be killed by Stoneman. We're just not!"

"I hope you're right. I'm tough to kill. A lot of men have tried and none have succeeded."

She ran her fingers across his bare torso. "But you have so many scars. Terrible scars from terrible wounds."

"You noticed."

She nodded. "Sure I did. I'm almost a doctor. Remember?"

"That's a good thing for us, Addie. Because I've got a bad feeling a lot of blood is going to be spilled and some of it . . . some of it may be my own."

"We'll make it. I told you that I'm tough. That I can shoot straight and, if I have to, I will stand by you and Father to the death."

"I just hope you don't have to," Longarm heard himself tell her.

Addie drained her wineglass, then went into her kitchen. In a cabinet she found a bottle of Kentucky mash. "This is premium stuff and it's more powerful than the kick of a Missouri mule."

"Do you drink that?" Longarm asked.

"A sip for luck and courage when I need it, but mostly I use it to kill germs."

"Let's give it a taste," Longarm said, abandoning his

wineglass. "After all that talk about long odds and Stone-man, I think we could use something stronger than wine."

"My sentiments exactly."

So they filled fresh glasses and raised them to each other.

"To life and love," she said.

"And to the end once and for all of Wade Stoneman," he added.

"That, too."

They drank, and both coughed and sputtered a little. Longarm was the first to stammer, "Gawd, this is pure alcohol!"

"Yes, it is," she admitted. "Kills those germs *real* good! So how about a toast to Pasteur, the man who came up with the Germ Theory?"

"I'll drink to the man," Longarm said, voice raw. "And then I'd like to up the ante and celebrate again in your bed, between your long and lovely legs."

Addie splashed more mash into their glasses and blushed. "By golly," she said with her voice a little husky from the fiery liquor, "I believe that you're a man worth fighting and dying for."

"Like your father?"

"Like my father."

Longarm nodded, and they drank their mash down neat.

"To bed!" she cried, grabbing his hand and nearly jerking him off his feet as she rushed back into her bed-room.

They threw themselves into a second bout of pas-sionate lovemaking. When it was finally over and they lay close together, Longarm said, "I never made love with a woman doctor before now."

"And I never had a tall, handsome marshal," she replied.

After that, they lay tight in each other's arms, each silently thinking about Buffalo Falls and wondering how they could possibly stop Wade Stoneman.

Chapter 5

Longarm and Addie arrived at the train station just minutes before the train was set to pull out for Cheyenne.
They found Marshal Billy Vail pacing up and down the
platform in a state of high anxiety.

"Well, there you are!" Billy said sarcastically. "Custis,
I'm so glad you could get out of bed and finally make it
down here to the station."

Longarm was in no mood for levity, so he nodded and
took the money that Billy handed him in a brown envelope. "How much?"

"Two hundred."

"I was hoping for at least four hundred," Longarm
said with a frown of disapproval. "Billy, you know that I
might have to hire a few men as well as a horse and outfit. On top of all that, I'm going to need to buy a good rifle and boxes of ammunition."

"How come you didn't bring your own rifle?" Billy
said, not pleased. "The new one we bought you when you
got in that big fix over in Santa Fe."

Longarm looked sheepish. "Well, if you have to

41

know, the last time I took it on an assignment, it was . . . was stolen."

Billy shook his head with disgust. "That's pathetic, Custis. You're a deputy United States marshal and you allowed someone to steal your new Winchester?"

"Dammit, Billy, I got distracted."

"By a woman, I'll bet."

Longarm looked away, confirming Billy's suspicion.

"Speaking of women," Longarm said, pocketing the cash and wanting to change the tone of the conversation. "This is my new friend, Miss Addie Hudson. Addie was the young lady that was mugged yesterday, so don't be thinking I beat her up and gave her both a split lip and a shiner."

Billy managed a tolerant smile. "Miss Hudson. I'm glad that my deputy could help you yesterday. Sorry that you had to go through such a bad experience."

"He's my hero," Addie said, using her good eye to wink at Longarm and then slipping her arm through his arm. "Marshal Vail, I'm sure that I don't have to tell you that you're very fortunate to have such a brave and resourceful deputy marshal."

Billy nodded. "He's one of a kind, all right. A real piece of work for certain. I don't have anyone else that I would dare send alone to Buffalo Falls. So let's just hope that we see him return safe and in good health."

"I'm going to do my best to see that is what happens," Addie said. "I'm a doctor, Marshal Vail. Even more to the point, I'm accompanying Marshal Long to Buffalo Falls."

"No!" Billy's response was instantaneous and instinctive. Probably embarrassed by his outburst, he lowered his voice. "I didn't mean to sound so forceful,

Miss Hudson, but Custis is going on a very difficult and dangerous assignment. I really don't think that you should—"

"I know all about the dangers he's up against," Addie said, cutting him off. "And while I don't want to shock you, I'm from Buffalo Falls."

Billy's jaw dropped. "Are you serious?"

"Absolutely. My father owns a ranch near that town and he's under attack from Wade Stoneman as are many others."

Billy glanced at Longarm, who nodded. "It's true, Billy. Miss Hudson is from Buffalo Falls. She's been living here in Denver for a few years studying to become a woman doctor."

"That's wonderful, Miss Hudson, but all the same I don't . . ."

He didn't get to finish because the locomotive's whistle blasted three times, drowning out his objection.

"Billy," Longarm said, picking up his bag as well as Addie's. "I tried hard to get Addie to stay here in Denver—or at least give me a week or two to sort things out in Wyoming. But Addie is a doctor, and furthermore, she knows the territory and the politics in Buffalo Falls. And she thinks that that telegram you received isn't from her father, but from someone else who is being bullied and railroaded by Stoneman. So I couldn't stop her from coming with me to Wyoming even if I tried."

"I don't like this," Billy said, looking from one of them to the other. "Custis, the last thing you need is to be worrying about Miss Hudson's health and safety."

"She's not only a doctor who knows the locals and the land," Longarm said, "but Miss Hudson assures me that she is a crack shot with either a gun or a rifle."

"That is remarkable," Billy said, not sounding convinced, "but she is still—"

"A woman," Addie said, finishing Billy's sentence. "So because I don't have the right . . . plumbing, you think I can't help but be a complication and hindrance to your deputy."

Billy was embarrassed. "No offense, Miss Hudson, but I just don't want to see either of you get hurt . . . or worse."

"I've been hurt before. Marshal Vail, my dear father is fighting not only for his ranch, but also his life. I could no more stay here in Denver than I could fly to the moon. So I'm sorry if you think I'm a threat or liability to your best deputy marshal, but I'm still going with him to oppose and bring down Wade Stoneman."

The locomotive suddenly jerked, and the sound of couplings crashing tight echoed all down the train. The conductor cupped his hands and shouted, "All aboard for Cheyenne, Wyoming!"

Billy's eyes shifted slowly from Longarm to Addie and back to Longarm, as if he thought he might never see either of them again. "Just . . . be careful," he pleaded as the train started moving. "Keep in close touch by telegraph and, if you need help, I'll send more agents!"

"I'll do that!" Longarm shouted as Addie swung up onto the Union Pacific train, and then he followed her onto the step. "And I'll probably need more money in the next week or two!"

"Custis, if you handle this Wade Stoneman mess, then I'll see that you get a big, fat monthly raise."

"Fair enough! But I'm still going to need more money to take care of business in Wyoming."

"I'll keep that in mind!"

"You do that!" Longarm called as the train pulled out of the station.

Billy nodded and waved, thinking it was very likely that his friend and best deputy marshal might not live long enough to spend the money he had already pocketed.

The trip up to Cheyenne across the rolling grasslands pocked with buffalo wallows was uneventful, and after the previous night of vigorous and frequent lovemaking, both Longarm and Addie slept in their seats nearly all the way north.

When the train pulled into the Cheyenne station, they disembarked and found a nice room at one of the best hotels in town, then ordered dinner brought to their door.

Later that evening, while sitting in an easy chair sipping an excellent brandy and smoking a much better grade of cigar than he did in front of his boss, Longarm asked, "How far away is Buffalo Falls?"

Addie thought a moment, then said, "As the crow flies, it's about one hundred fifty miles and it's northeast of us."

That was farther than Longarm had expected. "Is there a regular stagecoach to carry us up to Buffalo Falls?"

Addie shook her head. "There are supply wagons that also carry mail, leaving maybe once a week. I rode one of them down from our ranch when I left for Denver. But I don't know when and if it leaves on a regular schedule."

"In the morning after breakfast, we'll ask around and find out what we need to do. I'd rather take a stagecoach than ride a horse that many miles."

"I'd rather ride a horse," Addie said with a troubled smile as she rubbed a medicinal ointment on her knees.

"But I'll take either just so long as we get there as fast as possible."

Longarm studied her. "Your eye is looking a little better and the knees a little worse."

"They're just scabbed up. In two or three more days, the scabs will be gone and they'll look just fine. They are the least of all my concerns."

"You're pretty worried about your father, aren't you." It wasn't a question.

"Yes," she said. "I should have left Denver a month ago when I got Father's last letter." Addie took a deep swallow of the brandy they'd ordered and said, "What if he's already dead? What if Father was killed by Stoneman or one of Stoneman's hired guns!"

Longarm didn't know what to say in response. "If he's gone, Addie, it'll be one more nail in Stoneman's coffin."

"That's not much consolation."

"I know," Longarm said, coming over to pull her close and comfort her. "But since we don't know otherwise, let's just assume that your father is alive and holding on. If we have to travel a hundred fifty miles, we can do it in three or four days."

"Three," she said, "if we buy a pair of really good horses."

"All right," Longarm agreed. "We'll get up first thing in the morning and see if there is a stagecoach or wagon leaving for Buffalo Falls. If not, we'll buy a couple good horses and provision ourselves for a fast trip north."

"Are you much of a horseman?" she asked with a slight grin.

"I can keep up with you," he vowed. "But I'm no cowboy, and I'll get saddle sores and butt blisters traveling that far that fast."

Addie laughed. "You're *more* than a cowboy, Custis. My father is going to like you a lot . . . especially when he learns how you saved me and our money back in Denver."

Longarm put his drink on the table and yawned. "Addie," he said, "if we're going to travel far and fast over the next three days, I'm going to take advantage of our soft hotel bed and get a good night's sleep."

She managed to smile. "Maybe we should see how those bedsprings bounce before we start counting sheep."

"You up to it?" he asked in surprise.

"No," she said, "but the real anatomical question is . . . are *you* up for it?"

Longarm was wearing only his underwear and when he glanced down at his manhood, he saw that it was limp. "Not yet, Addie, but I'll bet you can take care of that shortcoming."

Addie came into his arms and her fingers were soft, but strong and insistent. In only a few minutes, the two of them were testing out the mattress and box springs, and all the worry and bad thoughts about Wade Stoneman vanished from their minds like leaves blowing in a strong Wyoming wind.

Chapter 6

Longarm and Addie got moving early the next morning. By eight o'clock, Longarm had learned that the next supply wagon bound for Buffalo Falls wasn't going north for five days.

"Too long for us to wait," he said to the friendly owner of Cheyenne's largest general store. "Mister, where can I buy a couple of good horses at a fair price?"

"Galloway's Stable," the man said without hesitation. "The owner, Mike Galloway, is honest and he treats people fair, although he thinks that he knows everything there is to know about anything and everything. Mind if I ask why you want to go to Buffalo Falls? From what I hear, it's not a healthy or happy place to be anymore."

Addie stepped forward. "This is Deputy Marshal Custis Long and he's come from Denver to investigate the illegal activities of Wade Stoneman. Custis used to work with Stoneman."

Longarm could have choked Addie, and yet he knew that it was his fault in not telling her that he really didn't like people knowing his business unless it was absolutely necessary. But like it or not, the cat was out of the bag so to speak, and Longarm felt sure that soon half of Cheyenne would learn who he was and why he'd been sent from Colorado.

As if sensing Longarm's displeasure at her blurting out the reason for their wanting to ride north, Addie tried to rectify her mistake. "But, mister, we'd appreciate it if you'd keep this information under your hat. Do that and it would make things easier for us both and maybe improve our chances of taking Stoneman down."

The store owner nodded with understanding. He was a man in his forties, short and bald, but still fit-looking and rather handsome. "Sure! I know how to keep a secret, and from what I've heard of Wade Stoneman, the last thing you want to do is give him any warning. So don't worry, I'll keep what you've told me in strict confidence."

"In that case," Longarm said, spotting a well-stocked gun rack behind the counter, "why don't you fix us up provisions for the trail? Also, I see that you carry quite a few rifles and shotguns."

"I take them in trade for supplies when people are down on their luck. People have to eat, but they don't necessarily have to own a rifle or shotgun."

Longarm leaned over the counter and studied the rack of weapons with serious interest. "Which is the best rifle in that rack?"

The man carefully took down a fine Winchester repeater. "This one is hardly used at all. I haven't test-fired it, but I'm sure it shoots straight and has no malfunctions. I'll bet it hasn't fired fifty rounds. At least, that's what the man that traded it in told me."

Longarm examined the rifle. "How much do you want for it?"

"Twenty-five dollars . . . and just to show you I'm a fair man, I'll throw in a full box of ammunition."

"Sold." Longarm looked to Addie. "What about you?"

"I've got a Colt and a derringer packed away in my valise, and I expect my father still has my favorite rifle waiting up at the ranch."

"Does he own a shotgun?" Longarm asked, spotting an extremely impressive shotgun on the store owner's gun rack.

"Why, no. Why should he?"

"No good reason, I guess," Longarm said. "But I like the peace of mind they can give a man who is outnumbered. Mister, how much for that fancy double-barreled shotgun with the light-colored stock?"

The store owner grinned. "Now *that* is a real crowd tamer and a mighty fine weapon that was made in some little country called Belgium . . . or maybe it was Spain. I forget. It's beautifully engraved, as you can see, and you won't find a finer shotgun anywhere, not even in Denver."

"Those barrels are big. What gauge?"

"It's an eight-gauge and I guarantee that it'll blow off the barn doors at each end and then knock down a couple of horses."

"Where'd you get a weapon like that?" Longarm asked, becoming even more interested in the beautiful shotgun.

"Glad you asked," said the man, taking down the shotgun and holding it with near reverence. "You see, there was a rich English gentleman here hunting game birds this summer. But the shotgun kicked him so hard that he said it nearly broke his right shoulder. He had

51

been shooting it on a guided hunt, and when he came to my store to unload that fine weapon, his arm was resting was in a sling and he couldn't hardly move his shoulder. That's why I purchased that fine sporting weapon for a fraction of its true value. Marshal, I'm willing to pass my good fortune on to you."

"You got shells for this little cannon?" Longarm asked, taking the shotgun and hefting it for balance, then checking the barrel and breech. It was far too beautiful to kill men, but it had really caught Longarm's eye and fancy. He wanted it very much.

"I do. Two boxes."

"How much do you have to have for it?" Longarm asked, doubting he could afford the weapon.

"Hmm, well, I sure don't want to give this beauty away, Marshal."

"How much," Longarm repeated.

"How about . . . how about this remarkable shotgun and two full boxes of shells for just sixty dollars."

Longarm whistled and shook his head. "Afraid that's a little rich for a working lawman."

"Marshal, this gun would easily bring a hundred dollars in Denver. Easily! And it would bring twice that much money back East."

The man was right. Longarm figured that, if he survived Buffalo Falls, he could take the impressive sporting weapon back to Denver and sell it for maybe a hundred fifty dollars. It would be a nice profit. Hell, that kind of profit would be worth a month's salary . . . if he could bear to part with such a beautiful shotgun.

"Mister, you're probably right, but I just don't know if I can afford it," he said more to Addie than to the store owner. "Provisions and a buying a horse, saddle, and that Winchester are taking up almost all of my travel money. If I spend another sixty dollars on top of all the rest for this shotgun, then I'll be pretty near busted."

"I'll buy it for you," Addie said without hesitation.

"Aw, I couldn't let you do that!"

"I'm afraid you're going to have to," Addie told him. "After all the money you saved me from losing in Denver, it's the least I can do. Besides, you just might need it to help me and my father against Wade Stoneman."

Longarm wasn't a man to take gifts, but in this case if he declined Addie's generous offer, he reckoned that it would be an example of a man being overcome by his foolish pride. "Okay," he said. "But when this is over, if we're still standing, then you can have the shotgun for your own."

"I wouldn't even want to think of shooting that cannon," Addie said with a grin. "It would knock me over and probably break my shoulder. Uh-uh, Custis. When we walk out of here, this shotgun is yours and yours alone."

"Fair enough," he said. "I'll come back for it and the Winchester when we get the horses bought," he told the store owner. "If you could have the provisions in a sack, we'll pay the damages just before we leave town."

The store owner was very happy. He'd already made more than an average day's sales in just a few minutes. "I'll have everything ready, Marshal. Do you need two bedrolls . . . or one?"

Longarm could see how the man's mind was running, and he started to say two, but Addie answered, "One good, heavy bedroll and a tarp will get us up to Buffalo Falls reasonably warm and dry."

"Good enough," the store owner said. "And how about

a little whiskey for the cold nights on the trail? You could get snowed on at this time of the year."

"Whiskey and a dozen cigars would be good," Longarm said. "And we'll want a couple of good-sized canteens and rain slickers to fit."

"Done!"

Longarm started to leave, but then turned and said, "How much do you reckon this will all cost us?"

The store owner frowned and toted up the figures in his head. "I'd say about one hundred twenty-five dollars, give or take five dollars."

"And that buys your word that you will keep silent about who I am and why I'm riding with this lady up to Buffalo Falls?" Longarm asked, his eyes piercing.

"Mister, you have my word on it! I'd keep my silence even if you didn't buy a dime's worth of hard rock candy."

"That's what I wanted to hear," Longarm said. "Where is Galloway's Stable?"

The man gave them directions and they went up the street. Addie said, "Do you think that man will keep your secret?"

"At least until we're out of Cheyenne," Longarm replied. "But I saw a ring on his finger, so he's married. Most likely, he'll have to tell his wife, and then she'll tell her friends who will tell their friends. I'd give it a day before the whole town knows my name and why we've ridden north."

Addie wasn't so sure that the store owner would break his promise. "You may be wrong and maybe that nice man will never say a word."

"Hope you're right." Longarm looked ahead and saw the livery. "You want me to do the pickin' and dickerin' for our horses?"

"I'll pick the horses," Addie said. "I think I know more about them than you do. After that, you can dicker over the price. If I think you've done well, I won't make a peep. But if I think you're getting taken, I'll have to step in and do the horse trading."

"Sounds like a plan," Longarm told her.

They bought the best two horses in Galloway's Stable. A red roan mare with a flaxen mane and tail for Addie, and a tall buckskin gelding for Longarm. They also bought saddles, bridles, halters, and blankets in addition to a couple of saddlebags.

"Where you headed?" Mike Galloway asked when the money changed hands.

"Maybe up into the Laramie Mountains," Longarm said.

"Are you serious?" Not waiting for or expecting an answer, Mike shook his head. "Man, those mountains will already be covered with snow. You go up there and you might get buried in the stuff. We get blizzards this time of year here in Wyoming."

"Then maybe we'll ride south to Old Mexico," Longarm told the liveryman because he didn't appreciate being lectured. "No blizzards any time of the year in Mexico."

Mike Galloway was a pugnacious-looking Irishman. He was a good and honest man, but he tended to be too free giving advice, and seemed a little on the self-important side for Longarm's liking.

"Mexico? Mister, are you serious?"

"Why not?" Longarm asked while Addie rolled her eyes.

"Why that's a long, long way!" the Irishman

exclaimed. "You couldn't get to Mexico in a month! Maybe three months. Why, you'd have to ride through Colorado, Oklahoma, maybe half of Nevada, and the corner of California. Hell, you'd have to ride all over the place to get there."

Longarm had to struggle to keep from chuckling. "You're right," he agreed with a feigned tone of fatalism. "I guess we'll just go down to Santa Fe, New Mexico, for the winter."

Galloway nodded. "That sounds a whole lot more sensible, mister. Old Santa Fe is a real nice town to winter up in. Real nice."

Longarm started to ask the know-it-all Irishman if he'd ever been in Santa Fe, but he knew the man would say he had and Longarm knew it would be a lie, so he just nodded.

They collected their newly purchased supplies, weapons, ammunition, and all the rest of their provisions and the bill totaled exactly $125. There was a nice-looking woman now behind the counter beside the store owner, and she was sure giving Longarm and Addie secretive looks, but trying not to stare.

"I told you," Longarm said as he tied down their newly purchased provisions and mounted the tall buckskin.

"Told you what?" Addie asked, swinging up on her red roan.

"That he'd tell his wife right away. And I'll bet you we don't get to the end of the street corner before that woman scoots out of the store and rushes off to tell *all* her female friends."

"You're cynical, Custis. Give us ladies a little credit for discretion."

"Whatever you say," Longarm replied. "But when we hit the end of the street, turn around in your saddle and I'll bet you a dollar that woman is out the door and on her way to gossip up a storm."

Addie didn't say anything, but when they reached the end of the street, she did twist around in her saddle for a moment.

"Well?" Longarm asked as they rode out of Cheyenne. "Was I right or not?"

"Don't get me riled up," Addie warned. "Because you're going to need a doctor, friend, and straight shooter before this is over."

Longarm suppressed a smile. He was right about the store owner's wife, of course. But Addie was also right about him needing her to watch his backside when they hit Buffalo Falls.

Chapter 7

Longarm and Addie really pushed their horses for the first two days, but on a cold and blustery third day while galloping across the rolling hills, Addie's roan mare stepped in a badger hole and did a complete somersault. Addie was pitched down hard on the prairie grass, and the mare had to struggle just to get back on her feet.

Longarm had been galloping stirrup to stirrup with the young woman, and when she and her horse tumbled, he reined up and then hurried back. Dismounting, he ran to the girl's side. "Addie!"

She was dazed, hurt, and moaning in confusion. Longarm cradled Addie's head in his lap and held her close, hoping that she hadn't sustained a fatal spine or internal injury. This was a bad place to have a wreck. There was a storm bearing down on them and not a farm or ranch house as far as the eye could see. If Addie was badly hurt, he had no idea where they could get medical help.

"Addie!" He shook her gently.

After a few minutes, she finally stirred, but when she looked up at Longarm, she seemed unable to focus.

"Addie, it's me, Custis! Can you hear me?"

"Yes," she whispered, sounding very tired and more than a little confused. "What . . . what happened?"

"Your mare went down into a badger hole and did a complete flip. I was riding just ahead and didn't see it happen, but you must have hit the ground very hard. Maybe your horse landed on you. I don't know. Can you move your hands and feet?"

Longarm's greatest concern was that Addie had suffered a terrible spine injury, leaving her paralyzed. But to his great relief, Addie was able to move her extremities. However, she said that her vision was blurred and she felt sick to her stomach.

"You're the doctor, but my guess is that you've suffered a real bad concussion," he said. "I've had a few of my own and I know that this will pass after you've had rest."

Addie tried to look around. "What about my poor horse?"

The mare had struggled up on three legs, and was hobbling over to join Longarm's buckskin. "Addie, I'm afraid that your mare is also hurt."

Tears filled her eyes. "Go see if she broke her leg, Custis. If she did, the poor horse will be in terrible pain and you'll have to shoot her."

"I'll get you some water to drink first."

Addie blinked and tried to grin. "Whiskey might make me feel better, but it wouldn't be what a doctor would order."

He eased her head back down on the dry brown grass. "I'll get my canteen and check on your horse."

"Dammit, Custis, I didn't see that badger hole."

"Some of them are covered over by grass or even

filled up a little from the summer rains," Longarm told her. "Hold tight and I'll be right back."

He rushed over to his buckskin and retrieved his canteen. Then he took a moment to catch the roan, who was now gently putting her injured left foreleg back down on the grass. Still, the mare didn't want it to take on very much of her weight. Longarm gathered the mare's reins and slowly led her around for a few moments. The mare's leg wasn't broken, but the horse was definitely lame.

Longarm tied the mare's reins to his saddle horn, and then led both horses back close to Addie, who was trying to sit up.

"Your roan's leg isn't broken," Longarm told her. "That's the good news. The bad news is that she's very lame."

Addie swore like a soldier. "Help me to sit up, Custis."

He eased her to a sitting position, and she closed one eye and said, "I'm seeing double so I do have a severe concussion."

"We'll make camp," he told her, shouting into a rising wind. "It's getting late in the day and these horses are worn out."

"I think that you're the one that's worn out."

"You got that right," he agreed. They both heard the clap of thunder in the darkening sky. "Addie, how much farther is it to Buffalo Falls or your ranch?"

"I was hoping that we could get there soon after dark. Can you see those low foothills off to the east?"

Longarm followed her gaze. "Yeah."

"Our ranch, the Lazy H, is right at the base of those hills."

"Where the hell is Buffalo Falls?"

"About five miles to the northeast of our ranch."

Since they were in trouble, Longarm wanted to make sure that he understood her correctly. "So your ranch is between us and the town?"

"Yes." She gripped Longarm's wrist. "Maybe we could ride double on your buckskin the rest of the way and still get to the ranch before midnight."

But Longarm shook his head. "If we did that, we'd have to leave the mare. She's in even more pain than you are."

"My fault. I was so intent on getting home and I wasn't even watching for badger holes."

Longarm knew that they needed shelter and that a storm was almost upon them. He studied the land and said, "There's a stand of cottonwoods about a mile or two farther ahead, and that means there must be running water. There's also bound to be enough cottonwood to give us fuel for a fire, and we've got rain slickers and plenty of food."

"Is that rumbling thunder I hear so close, or is the sound coming from my aching head?" Addie asked.

"It's thunder. The sky is darkening, and I'm afraid that we're going to get drenched before too much longer."

"Could be snow and not rain," Addie said, shivering. "It's not going to be a good night to be camping out here on the short grass."

"I know that," Longarm told her. "But you're in no condition to travel and neither is your mare. Maybe by morning, you'll both be able to go on."

"We'll have to be ready," Addie said. "I left the main wagon road way back this morning and cut straight across the range to shorten the distance to our ranch. Nobody will come along this way and help us out here in these rolling hills."

"We'll make out fine," Longarm said. "I'm going to lift you up on my gelding. Do you think you can hang on to the saddle horn until we reach the cottonwoods?"

"I think so," she said, shaking her head as if to clear her vision. "But if I start to fall, then tie me to your saddle."

Longarm hoisted Addie into his saddle, and then took a few minutes to shorten his stirrups so that she could ride easier. He collected the mare's reins as well as those of his own horse, and set out leading them to the distant cottonwoods. The wind was getting stronger and the dark thunderheads seemed to be bearing down on them with bad intentions.

Longarm wasn't even sure that he could make it to the cover of the trees, but he sure meant to try.

Longarm had underestimated the distance to the cottonwoods by at least a mile. And by the time he led Addie and the two horses into the shelter of those big, leafless trees, the wind was moaning and sleet was starting to pelt him in the face. Bare tree limbs were flailing wildly, and the wind was now a steady and icy blast coming all the way down from Canada.

The stand of cottonwoods did flank a creek, and Longarm led the way down into the wash, where there was at least some shelter from the driving wind and sleet. He tied the horses in the thickest of the trees to give them shelter, and then he pulled Addie from his saddle and carried her along the waterway, searching both banks for cover.

He got lucky when he found a cut-out place under the bank. He laid Addie down and used his bare hands to enlarge what was going to have to be their night's shelter. Afterward, he dragged limbs and logs over to help make a stout windbreak. Pulling Addie as far under the freshly enlarged cutback as he could, Longarm paused to assess their situation. It wasn't good. Wasn't good at all, but it was far better than being caught in this storm on the exposed prairie.

Addie was shivering and slipping in and out of consciousness. Longarm unsaddled their horses and covered Addie with horse blankets, then gathered as much dry wood and grass as he could get before everything around them was drenched. After striking four matches, he finally was able to cup his hands and get a few blades of grass to burn along with some brittle little branches. After that, it wasn't difficult to get a good fire crackling.

Longarm left Addie and barged back out in the storm to make sure that their horses were securely tied. He gave them handfuls of grain and hoped they would huddle up and not suffer too badly on this freezing and miserable Wyoming night.

He used his rain slicker to cover part of the opening to his little cave under the stream bank, and dragged all their provisions as well as his Winchester and the shotgun under its cover. Satisfied that he'd done everything possible to weather this sudden storm, he finally squeezed back under the shelter bank shivering violently.

Whiskey.

He remembered that the store owner in Cheyenne had sold them whiskey and that he and Addie hadn't drunk all that much of it on their first two nights out. Longarm found the whiskey and a dry cigar. He took a deep swallow of the liquor, and then lit his cigar in the campfire that was now burning brightly not a foot from where he huddled.

"Could be worse," he said, blowing smoke out in the cold wind and sleet and watching it disappear in an instant. "Could be one hell of a lot worse."

"Not much," Addie said, startling him.

Longarm turned to the woman, who was buried under horse blankets. "You're awake again."

"Yes. How about a pull on that bottle?"

"You're the doctor," he said.

"That's right, and whiskey is what I'm prescribing for my throbbing headache."

Addie took a generous swallow, then a second, and lay back against the dirt bank. She stared at the fire a moment and said, "Funny, but this isn't the first time that I've been huddled under a cutback like this."

"No?" Longarm asked. Addie's voice was a little slurred, but not so much that he couldn't understand her words. "What happened? Did you get caught in another storm?"

"Uh-uh," she said. "One summer when I was about fifteen, I was riding out on the range by myself searching for strays. It was a nice enough day, but this one big dark cloud was overhead, and suddenly a bolt of lightning shot out of it and caused a prairie fire." Addie shivered. "Have you ever been caught in one of those, Custis?"

"Can't say that I have. I've heard stories about them, though. They can really move fast. I've heard that, if they're being pushed by a hard wind, they can outrun any living thing."

"You bet they can! And this one was coming straight for me pushed by a stiff wind. I knew that I couldn't flank it, so I set my horse to running away and we raced for our lives. But I hadn't gone a mile when I realized that my horse wasn't going to get me out of the prairie fire's way."

Addie's voice caught in her throat and she was staring at the flames as if they were the prairie fire of long ago. "That fire was gaining on us and my horse was starting to falter."

"What saved you?" Longarm finally asked.

"A riverbed like this."

She seemed to snap out of her reverie, and gazed hard through the flames toward the opposite bank of their streambed. "It was deeper and wider than this one, but it was there all the same. I bailed off my horse and jumped down into the water, then crawled up and under the bank. It wasn't three or four minutes later that the fire hit the riverbed and jumped right over the top of me. It sounded like a runaway train."

"Was it pretty hot?"

"Nope. All the time I was down under that bank, I was clawing at the dirt and burrowing in deeper and deeper. The prairie fire passed right on over the top and kept racing on for miles. Burnt two homesteads and families to ashes. Fortunately, our ranch wasn't in its path, or it would have wiped us out just like those other folks."

"And what about your horse?"

Addie swallowed hard. "He . . . he was burned to death. I found what was left of him and my saddle about a half mile away. I've always felt terrible about abandoning that animal."

"You had no choice," Longarm told her. "You did the only thing you could do under the circumstances."

"I know. My father told me the exact same thing over

and over. But it still hurts all these years later. He was a good pony, and I should have shot him before I jumped down into that riverbed and started digging for my life. All I was selfishly thinking about was saving my own life."

Longarm nodded at his flickering campfire and listened to the howling wind. "I know what you mean about being selfish at times," he said. "And I honestly doubt there is anyone who doesn't have some regrets. Who hasn't thought about what they did and realized that they might have done things a little better. But looking back and having regrets is a waste of time, or so I've found it to be."

Addie studied him. "Do you have many regrets?"

Cutis dipped his chin. "More than I can count. Mostly about the war and all the men I killed. They were not much more than boys mostly."

"Who would have killed you if you didn't kill them first," Addie reminded him.

"I like to think that was the case," Longarm replied, staring into the fire and taking another pull on his bottle. "Yes, sir, I'd sure like to think that was the case."

Addie reached out and touched him on the sleeve. "If you hadn't been thinking quickly when I was spilled by the roan mare, we could still be out on the open prairie fighting for our lives in this early winter storm. You saved me again, Custis. That's twice now."

He looked at her and smiled. "And I saved myself."

"Maybe one of these days I'll save your life for a change."

"You have my permission," he said with a short laugh. "Yes, ma'am, you sure do have my permission on that score."

Longarm, with a little help from Addie, finished off the whiskey and then his cigar. He pulled up the collar of his coat and saw that the driving sleet had turned to snow. But protected from the wet and wind inside their little earthen shelter, they were warm and in no danger.

No, he thought, *this storm isn't going to do us any harm, but the real danger is waiting just up ahead in Buffalo Falls.*

Chapter 8

The storm lasted until just before dawn, and when Longarm crawled out from under the riverbank, the snow was almost two feet deep. The air was cold and clear, and Longarm figured they could make good time reaching Addie's ranch this morning. Their horses were eager to eat the last of the grain that Longarm had bought in Cheyenne, and Longarm walked the roan mare around, pleased to note that her limp was much less pronounced.

"Our horses are still here?" Addie asked when Longarm returned to her shelter.

"Yep. And your mare is still limping, but not nearly as badly. I'll saddle both horses and we can be on our way to your ranch."

"I'm ready," Addie told him even though her head was still aching. "It seems that we weathered this storm in good shape."

"Let's just hope we can weather the storm in Buffalo Falls," he told her. "When was the last time you heard from your father?"

"About a month ago. He sent a letter asking me to

empty our savings account in Cheyenne and borrow whatever money I could and come on home."

"Did he say that he felt he was in real danger from Wade Stoneman?"

Addie bit her lower lip. "Yes. In the letter he said that Stoneman had offered him a ridiculously low price for our ranch, and when that low offer was turned down, Stoneman become threatening."

"A lot could have happened in a month," Longarm told her. "Let's just hope that your father is still alive and unharmed."

"He'd be tough to kill," Addie said, clearly worried. "And he had a man working for him who was a former Indian scout and buffalo hunter. I met him once and his name was Casey. No last name, just Casey. But I could tell he was tough and not the kind to duck out of a fight."

Longarm digested this information without comment as he helped Addie onto her mare and then mounted his buckskin. He eyed the low hills in the distance, and they set off at a steady walk. The sun was up, there was no wind, and Longarm had the feeling that most of this snow would be gone in a day or two unless there was another storm.

They arrived at the ranch just before noon and there wasn't a soul in sight. The log farmhouse was large with a nice porch, and there were several barns and corrals. But it was very quiet. No horses. No dogs. No people. Just a penned red rooster and a few hens that got excited when they saw Longarm and Addie riding into the ranch yard.

"It's so quiet that it's spooky," Addie said, not waiting for Longarm to help her down from her horse. "Maybe my dad is taking a nap. Father!"

There was no sound other than the cackling of hungry chickens in their pen.

She walked to the porch and gripped the rail. "Father! It's Addie!"

Still no sound. Longarm looked around and he had a bad feeling in his gut. He didn't want to share that feeling with Addie, so he said, "Maybe your father and Casey went off to gather cattle or to get supplies."

"Or to Buffalo Falls to get supplies," Addie said, taking an unsteady step. "But Father always had a big, unfriendly yard dog or two hanging around this place to scare off coyotes or people who showed up when he was gone. Custis, this doesn't feel right to me. Something is terribly wrong!"

"Here," Longarm said, "let me help you up these porch steps."

They climbed the porch and went to the front door. Longarm pounded on the door and tried the handle. It was locked. He moved to the side and peered in through a glass window.

"I don't see anything, Addie. No one is home."

"There's a hideout key under that flowerpot," she told him, pointing. "Please get it and unlock the door."

Longarm drew his six-gun before he went through the front door. The smell of rotting food struck him forcefully, and he had a bad feeling deep down in the pit of his stomach. A table was overturned and a drinking glass was shattered on the living room floor.

Addie stared at these things, and her voice sounded frightened when she called, "Father!"

Longarm cautiously moved toward the stench. He

had smelled death many times, but this was not the decay of a human body. Stepping into the kitchen, he saw cooked food that was only half-eaten on the table. A glass of water was half-full. A door leading out the rear of the house was half-opened. It was so cold inside the house that they could see their breath.

"Oh, my God!" Addie whispered, her hand flying to her mouth as she took in the scene. "Something terrible must have happened."

Longarm thought so too when he stepped out of the back door following black drops of crusted blood. He followed the drops into some trees, and then he saw the shape of a man lying under the fresh snow.

Addie saw the still outline at the exact same moment. "Father!"

Longarm tried to grab Addie and hold her back, but she got around him too quickly, and then she was on her knees beside the body scraping off the mantle of snow.

"Oh, no!" she screamed. "Father, no!"

It appeared to Longarm that the man had been dead for at least a week. Longarm stood back and watched as Addie stroked the remains of her father. He could see two prominent bullet holes in Mr. Hudson's back, and a third shot in the back of his head that had probably been fired from directly above. This head shot had exited the rancher's gaping mouth. About ten feet away, there was a large brown dog that had also been shot to death. Its lips were pulled back from its fangs in a silent death snarl.

Longarm just stood quietly for a few minutes letting Addie grieve. Then he pulled the girl up and held her close and let her cry her heart out. Finally, he said,

"Addie, there's nothing we can do for him now. Let's go back inside."

"I can't just leave Father out here!"

"I'll find a tarp or blanket and carry his body into the barn where it will be safe. We can bury your father here on the ranch or take him into town, but we need to do it right away."

Addie's face was wet with tears. "He'd want to be buried next to Mother. We have a little cemetery here on the ranch."

Longarm nodded and helped Addie inside. He hoped that she didn't notice the blood, but she did. Her face was pale with grief. Longarm thought she might handle this tragedy better if she had something to do, so he said, "Maybe you could get a fire burning in the hearth. It's freezing in the house."

She nodded dumbly, and Longarm saw a wool blanket draped over an easy chair. He gathered the blanket and went back outside. After a few minutes, he had the decomposing body wrapped up and he carried it to the closest barn. The body would have been in awful shape and nearly impossible to move had it not been freezing cold.

Longarm gently placed the body on the floor of the barn, and closed the doors on his way out. He wasn't looking forward to returning to the house and facing Addie, but they had to accept the sad fact that they'd arrived here too late.

Longarm spent two difficult hours that afternoon gouging out a proper grave in the half-frozen ground. Addie was grief-stricken and silent as they laid her father to rest beside her mother's grave. She read from the family Bible, and then Longarm shoveled in dirt and filled the grave while Addie wept bitter tears.

Afterward, they sat in the front room of the ranch house and mostly just looked out the window and wondered aloud who had killed Addie's father.

"It must have been Wade Stoneman or one of his men," Addie said. "No one else would do such a thing to Father. He was well respected and a friend to all in this cattle country. I can't tell you how many times he went to the aid of one of his neighbors."

"I'll go into Buffalo Falls and start asking questions," Longarm vowed. "What about this hand called Casey?"

Addie looked up suddenly. "Yes, what about him? I'd completely forgotten that he was supposed to be helping protect my father."

"Do you think he might have betrayed your father? Perhaps even shot him?"

"I don't know," Addie admitted. "I hardly knew the man, and only met him the last time I was here visiting last Christmas. Casey seemed like a good and trustworthy man. I know that I was relieved when he swore to me that he'd stay on and help Father fend off Wade Stoneman and anyone else who came to take the Lazy H by force."

"Maybe he was also shot to death," Longarm said. "They might have ambushed Casey out on the range when he was chasing strays by himself."

She shook her head. "I just don't know. Casey gave me the impression of being a very capable and cautious man. Someone who wouldn't be shot or killed without a fight."

"If they cut him off from this ranch house, he wouldn't

have had much of a chance against three or four good riflemen," Longarm reasoned. "They'd have shot his horse and then closed in around him. There wouldn't be a lot that a single man could do out in this open country if he werc badly outnumbered and his horse was down."

"Yes. I can see that you're right."

"On the other hand, Casey might have been the one who shot your father in the back. He could have easily done that if your father trusted the man."

Her eyes widened. "But why would Casey do a thing like that?"

"Money," Longarm said without hesitation. "It's entirely possible that Wade Stoneman made Casey an offer that he just couldn't turn down. Even good men have sold out and been bought when the price was high enough. You didn't know the man. He might not have been as good or as loyal as you wanted to believe."

"I hope to God that's not true."

"But it might be," Longarm insisted. "I'll nced a real good description of Casey before I go to Buffalo Falls. And anything else you can tell me about him."

"I'm afraid that I really don't know anything about the man. He didn't talk much. It wasn't that he was unfriendly, he was just real quiet. Father said he liked that about Casey."

"Describe the man," Longarm said. "If he was paid to betray your father and kill him, he might still be in Buffalo Falls, and I want to get the drop on him before he figures out who I am and why I've come all the way from Denver."

"Well," Addie said, trying to pull herself together and concentrate, "Casey was about your age. Mid-thirties. He was shorter than you, but probably stood almost six feet in his boots. I remember he had a prominent scar on his right cheek. He wore a full beard, but you could see that scar because the whiskers that had come through along the scar were snow-white."

"That ought to be a pretty easy thing to spot. Was Casey stocky or slender?"

"Slender, but broad-shouldered. He favored a floppy brown hat, and the one side of the brim was pinned up to the crown while the other drooped partway over the scarred side of his face."

"Did he wear high-heeled cowboy boots?"

"Yes, and they were black. And he wore a gun in a nice black holster resting on his right hip. I would describe Casey as a hard and dangerous-looking man. He had very intense brown eyes and when he moved he had a slight limp, but it didn't seem to slow him down any. Father said he was an excellent cowboy and a complete loner. Said he never talked about his past. Father didn't mind that he was so quiet. He said *he* could talk enough for both of them and the main thing was that Casey was sober, hardworking, and dependable."

"Good enough," Longarm said. "With that description, I'd recognize him in an instant."

"It's late in the day," Addie said, looking back out the window. "Custis, why don't we both go into Buffalo Falls first thing tomorrow morning? You've had a hard day and I would appreciate your company very much."

"I really need to go to town, Addie. But I'll be back tonight. You need to rest and get to feeling better," he told her. "You cracked your head pretty hard when that roan mare took a spill. I'd rather you stayed here and recuperated."

Addie's eyes showed her worry. "But what if you get into serious trouble and need me?"

Longarm went over and hugged Addie. "If I get into something that I can't handle, then I'll just hightail it out of Buffalo Falls and come back here for reinforcements. You said it was only five miles away."

"That's right. You'll see the wagon road heading north and you can't get lost. In fact, you'll see the town pretty quick once you leave the ranch."

"Where are your father's cattle and horses?"

Addie shook her head. "I don't know. We should have seen some of them on the way here. I . . . I just don't know."

"I'll find out what happened to them and your father."

"Promise me you'll be very careful?"

"Yeah," he said, "I promise."

Addie looked back out the window. "Keep a close eye on the weather, Custis. In this country and at this time of year, storms can come upon you in a hurry."

Addie needed a lot of reassuring and that was to be expected. "I'll keep one eye out for trouble and one eye out for bad weather."

"Good. I'll have supper waiting."

"Don't bother, Addie. I'll find a place in town to eat."

"Dolly's is a good place. She's nosy and will try and find out everything she can about you, including if you want a little upstairs dessert to go with your supper."

He winked and grabbed his hat. "I'll decline some of that Dolly dessert."

"You'd better," Addie warned. "Also, there's a man that I know you can trust named Rollie Reed. He's a saddle and harness maker and you'll see his shop there in town."

Longarm knew that he would need someone to talk to that he could trust not to be in Stoneman's pocket. "Would Rollie confide in me about Wade Stoneman?"

"I think he would," Addie said after careful thought. "So long as Rollie doesn't think that it would get him shot."

"I'll drop by and pretend I'm interested in a new bridle or something. And I'll damn sure ask him if he knows about your father and about this fella named Casey." Longarm headed for the door. "Addie, just rest and get to feeling better. I'm going to need your help."

"I'm still seeing double, but maybe that will be gone tomorrow."

"I hope so. Otherwise, I'm going to make you use that big double-barreled shotgun. Two images and two barrels, you can shoot one and then the other barrel if we get in an awful fix."

It was meant as a joke, and it brought a smile to Addie's lips. That was the best that Longarm could do right now, so he left the house and set about on his way to find out what trouble awaited in Buffalo Falls.

Chapter 9

Longarm was surprised at the size of Buffalo Falls. Its main street boasted no less then two dozen stores and businesses, and there were perhaps fifty or sixty residences, many with large willow or cottonwood trees shading their neat yards. There was also an impressive bank that had Stoneman's name attached in gold lettering, and a handsome two-storied hotel made of brick. Longarm saw a newspaper office, and even a millinery store for the ladies.

It was clear that Wade Stoneman had made a big impact on the town because several of the most prominent buildings bore his name.

"Wade has come a long way up since I knew him in Denver," Longarm said to himself, "but I'll bet his gains here are all ill-gotten."

Longarm didn't want to chance upon Stoneman. Not yet. First, he wanted to poke around awhile and see what kind of information he could get on the man and also what the general feeling was about him. If Stoneman was the most prominent landowner in this town and

the wealthiest, then he would have his share of support-
ers as well as detractors.

It was the detractors that most interested Longarm.

He spotted a shop with a sign that read REED'S SAD-
DLES AND HARNESS. Longarm decided that this was
probably as good a place as any to stop and try to learn
something useful.

He tied his buckskin at the hitching rack and dismounted. Before leaving the Lazy H Ranch, he'd found
an old bridle in the Hudson barn that was in sad shape,
and now he took it inside the saddlery. If anyone was
watching him, it would seem as if he had a legitimate
purpose for the visit.

"Hello," a nice-looking man with brown hair and
blue eyes said, looking up from his bench, which was
covered with scraps of leather, knives, heavy needles,
and other leather-working tools. "What have you got
there?"

Longarm held up a bridle that had seen better days.
"It's in pretty bad shape, I'm afraid."

Rollie Reed got up from his three-legged bench stool
and came over to examine the bridle. He frowned.
"Mister, does this old bridle somehow mean something
real special to you?"

"Nope," Longarm replied.

"Then I wouldn't recommend having it repaired. The
leather is dried and cracked. I could restitch it and it
would work for a while, but I wouldn't trust it not to
break before long. I can sell you a new bridle for not
much more than I'd have to charge you to fix this one."

"Thanks," Longarm said, taking the bridle back. He
spied a trash can in the corner, and pitched the old bridle into the can.

"Good shot," Reed said. "Want to see what I have already made and for sale, or would you rather I custom-make you a bridle? Maybe a real nice one with your name or initials stamped into the leather."

Longarm figured it was time to come clean and state the real purpose of his visit. "Actually, I didn't come here for leatherwork, although I sure admire these saddles you've made and are for sale."

"Then why are you here?" Rollie Reed studied him closely, and then folded his arms across his chest.

"I'm a friend of Addie Hudson and a deputy United States marshal out of Denver."

Reed started with surprise. "How is Addie—I mean Miss Hudson?"

"I'm afraid that she's not so good," Longarm said, glancing over his shoulder to make sure no one was outside and the door was closed. "Addie and I arrived at her ranch yesterday and discovered that her father had been shot to death out behind the ranch house."

"Oh, dear God!" Reed whispered. "I was wondering why Mr. Hudson didn't come in on Tuesday. That's when he told me he was going to pick up a new set of braided rawhide reins that I'd made for him."

"He was shot twice in the back and once in the head," Longarm said. "And his dog was shot to death not far from his body."

Rollie Reed was obviously shaken, and he went back to slump on his stool. "And you came to town find out who did it?"

"When Addie and I left Denver, Mr. Hudson was probably still alive. But someone killed him and drove off all his horses and cattle. I'm here to find out if it was Wade Stoneman."

"What makes you think it might be him?"

"Our Denver office got an anonymous telegram saying that Stoneman was taking over this town and its most profitable ranches. That he started out as your marshal, shot four prominent townspeople, and is now not only your mayor, but also the owner of your only bank and a powerful land company."

"All true," Reed said, nervously watching his front door. "Wade Stoneman is a very ambitious man, and he makes it difficult for anyone to oppose him."

"I know Stoneman all too well," Longarm said. "When I first signed on as a federal officer, I was assigned to work under Wade Stoneman. The man took a liking to me and showed me how he got things done."

Reed somberly nodded. "And?"

"And how he got things done wasn't by the book," Longarm said. "In fact, Stoneman operated by his own rule of law. He was the law unto himself, and pretty soon that got back to the chief marshal's office in Denver and he was put under surveillance."

"He's a killer without a conscience," Reed hissed, lowering his voice as if there were someone pressing an ear to one of his outer walls. "He can't be stopped."

"That's not true," Longarm argued. "I've been sent to investigate and stop him."

"You and what army?"

Longarm almost smiled. "Just me. But right now, I'm interested in who murdered Addie's father and stole all his livestock."

"That would be Stoneman."

"You didn't even have to think about that very hard," Longarm said. "Do you have any proof?"

"Not unless you find Hudson cattle and horses on

Stoneman's ranch, which adjoins the Lazy H Ranch." Reed paused a moment. "But even if you did that, Stoneman would just say that the cattle and horses wandered onto his place. He'd feign surprise that Mr. Hudson was dead, and you wouldn't have any evidence to arrest him."

"What about the man that worked for Hudson?"

"You mean Casey?"

"That's right."

Reed shook his head. "Casey is a tough man. He is someone that you just don't want to cross."

"Is he still around?"

"Oh, yes. He works for . . . who else . . . Wade Stoneman."

"Then maybe he killed Mr. Hudson."

"He might well have," Reed agreed. "Casey doesn't talk much. He doesn't have to warn people about himself. All you have to do is look into his eyes and you know that he'd kill you without hesitation."

"Where can I find him?"

"Casey is in and out of Buffalo Falls pretty often. But he's probably working most of his time on Stoneman's cattle ranch. It's about two miles to the west of the Hudson place. But I sure wouldn't go out there if I were you, Marshal."

"Why?"

"Well, you look like a man who values your own life, and I'd just hate to see Addie lose another person she cares about. And speaking about her, how is she holding up?"

"As well as you might expect."

Rollie Reed shook his head. "I was in love with her all the time that we were growing up, but my parents

83

were poor and her family was comparatively well-off with so much good grassland. Anyway, she was above me and when she left to go see if she could learn to be a doctor, I even thought about following her to Denver and setting up a business like this one."

"Maybe you should have," Longarm said. "Denver can always use another good saddle maker."

"I realize that now," Reed said. "I should have gone to Denver and kept after her until she either told me to drop dead or that she had finally fallen in love with me and wanted to be my wife."

Rollie shook his head and smoothed the rawhide tree of a saddle he was about to cover. After a moment, he glanced up at Longarm. "I suspect that you and Addie are in love, huh?"

"I don't know. We haven't known each other more than a couple of days. Addie was being mugged near my office in Denver and I happened to be in the right place at the right time."

"You arrested the mugger?"

"Muggers," Longarm corrected. "And they resisted arrest, so they got a one-way ticket to the undertaker's parlor."

"Jesus!" Rollie Reed whispered. "You sound like you learned pretty well from Wade Stoneman."

"In the case of those muggers, it was self-defense," Longarm replied. "You either kill a man or he kills you. Stoneman didn't operate that way. He shot first, and then didn't need to ask questions later."

"Addie should have stayed in Denver where she was safe."

"If you know her at all, you know that she's a fighter

and she'd never stay away from Buffalo Falls out of fear. And besides, she intends to practice medicine here."

"Yeah, that was her dream. That and helping her father work their ranch."

Longarm studied the young man. "After Addie left a few years ago, did you ever get married?"

"No."

"Because of Addie?"

"Is it that obvious?"

Longarm shrugged his broad shoulders. "It seems that she also has feelings for you."

"Now what makes you think that?" Reed quickly asked.

"She said you were about the only one in Buffalo Falls that I could trust and that you'd tell me everything you know so long as it didn't get you murdered."

"She said that?"

"Yes. And that tells me that she not only likes you, but trusts you."

Rollie snorted. "Yeah, I know that. But she doesn't *love* me."

"Maybe that will come in time. Both of you are smart and capable young people, and yet neither of you has gotten married. Think about it."

Rollie picked up a piece of leather and studied it while deep in thought. "I didn't know that her father had been murdered. When Casey rode into town four or five days ago, I just figured that he and Mr. Hudson had had a falling-out. And given that Casey is a tough man, I wasn't surprised that Stoneman put him on the payroll."

"So do you think that Casey is the one that murdered Mr. Hudson?"

"I have no idea," Reed said, "but he's sure capable of doing it."

"Yeah," Longarm said, "that's what Addie said, too."

"What are you going to do now, Marshal?"

Longarm thought about that for a moment. "I guess I'll go to Dolly's and get something to eat, then mosey around town for a while. I'll have a beer or two at the local saloons and learn what I can about Stoneman and his operation."

"Once people discover that you're a federal law officer, you're going to have a big bull's-eye target stitched to the middle of your back."

"It's happened before," Longarm said. "If you can help Addie or me in any way, I'd appreciate it."

"I hear things," Rollie Reed admitted. "Cowboys and townspeople both come in here and like to talk. They sit around my potbellied stove and drink coffee or whiskey from their flasks and watch me work the leather."

"Have you heard anything I can use?"

"I know that Stoneman is after the Lazy H Ranch. He's made no bones about the fact that it's his next priority. It's got the best water and grass for miles around. And even more important, the Lazy H butts up against *his* ranch, which makes it even more valuable to the man."

"I don't think that Addie would ever sell to that man."

"She might not have any choice," Reed said. "Best thing she could do is to take what money she can get and go find another town where they need and will accept a woman doctor."

Longarm stared at the saddle maker for a moment, then asked, "If you thought that someone murdered your father, would you just pack up and leave with your tail between your legs?"

Reed froze. "No," he said quietly, "I wouldn't. I'd get a gun and I'd find a way to kill the sonofabitch before he killed me."

"Can you handle a gun?"

"Why do you ask? You looking for a posse?"

"No," Longarm replied. "But it's always good to know what a friend is capable of in a bad pinch."

"I'm plenty capable," Reed said without sounding like he was bragging. "And if it comes to that and it's you and Addie against Stoneman and his gunnies, then you call on me and I'll come running."

"You really do love that girl."

"Yeah," he admitted, "I really do. But don't take that to mean I want *you* dead, Marshal."

"I won't," Longarm reassured him as he was leaving.

"You watch out for Dolly!"

Longarm turned in the doorway. "Why do you say that?"

"Because I got a strong feeling that Dolly will take a shine to you. Also, she's got not only the biggest pair of tits in Buffalo Falls, but also the biggest mouth. Anything you say to her can and will be repeated for everyone to hear."

"Addie told me Dolly loved to gossip," Longarm said, "but she forgot to mention that Dolly had a pair of big tits."

"They're fit for a milking cow, only not so hairy."

Longarm laughed out loud. "Rollie, are you telling me about those big tits from firsthand experience?"

It was the saddle maker's turn to chuckle. "See you later, Marshal."

"I'd appreciate it if you didn't call me that. Not yet. People around here will learn who I am soon enough."

"I understand."

Longarm closed the door and headed for Dolly's and some eagerly awaited food.

Chapter 10

"Well, hello, handsome! Where on earth did you come from?" Dolly exclaimed, bold brown eyes raking Longarm's body from head to toe. "Sit yourself down and let Dolly serve you."

There were at least a dozen other men in the little café, and Longarm could feel his cheeks burn as some of them chuckled with amusement. But there was nothing to do but sit and endure Dolly, so Longarm took a seat near the front window.

"You look lobo-wolf hungry to me," Dolly said, brushing back a strand of long dark hair. "And this is the place to get taken real good care of."

"How about a cup of coffee, a steak, potatoes, and whatever else you can cram on a plate?"

"Sure, darlin'!" She leaned over the table so that her massive breasts were straining at the neckline and almost in Longarm's face. "And I'll bet a man like you wants his meat hot, juicy, and pink."

"I like my steak medium-rare and I like mashed potatoes with lots of gravy," he replied.

"What kind of dessert do you hunger for, mister?"

"What kind have you got?"

"I got pies, cakes, and sweet-tasting *me*!" She poured him a cup of steaming coffee.

This remark caused the entire café to erupt in laughter. Longarm was embarrassed and angry. He scowled and looked around at the other patrons. "Maybe you boys better wipe those grins off your faces before I teach you some manners."

"You gonna do that all by your lonesome, stranger?"

Longarm turned to a big man with a busted nose and lantern jaw and replied, "That's right."

"Stranger, I think you're all talk."

Longarm picked up his hot coffee and hurled it right into the man's ugly face, causing him to let out a howl of pain. Before the man could clear his eyes, Longarm hit him with a straight right cross that sent him flying out of his chair. The man tried to get up, but when he saw Longarm's expression, he gave up that poor idea.

"Anybody else think I'm all talk?" Longarm challenged.

No one moved and no one was laughing anymore. Satisfied, Longarm sat down and placed his napkin in his shirt. "Okay, Dolly, snap to it! I'm hungry!"

"Yes, sir!" she said, no longer having fun. "I'll put the meat right on the fire."

"Good. But before you do that, pour me another cup of coffee. I seem to have spilled the first one." Longarm lit a cigar and smoked in silence as he watched the man he'd punched being helped to the door. Once he and his friends were gone, it wasn't long before conversation returned to the café and things were back to normal.

Fifteen minutes later, Dolly brought him a thick steak

bathed in fried onions alongside potatoes and gravy. She hesitated a moment and said, "Listen, stranger, I didn't mean to tease you so bad. But everyone in Buffalo Falls knows I like to have a little fun and don't mean nothin'. Not really. And I apologize for any offense I caused you."

"If this steak is as good as it looks, all is forgiven."

Dolly smiled and wiped up a little spilled coffee. Leaning close, she said in a low, soft voice, "But mister, you are a handsome sonofabitch, and if you ain't married or anything, you'd really like my *special* dessert served in a special place."

Again, he took a measure of the Dolly's big tits, and then he couldn't help but give her a slight smile. "Don't tempt me. I've come here with Addie Hudson."

"Oh," Dolly said, not hiding her disappointment. "And next you'll tell me that you and she get hitched."

"No. I'm just . . . a friend of hers."

"I'll bet you are. Well, if you need another friend, you keep me in mind. All right?"

"I'll keep that in mind." Longarm cut into his steak and took a bite. It was delicious and when he looked up, there were those huge tits staring him in the face again.

"You like them?" she asked with a sexy grin.

"Yeah, I sure do," he answered. "And the steak isn't bad either."

Dolly beamed and went to serve her other customers.

Longarm was one of the last customers to finish, and he waited until Dolly was starting to clean up behind the counter before he got up from his table and went over to speak to her in a low voice that couldn't be overheard. "Could I have a few minutes?" he asked.

She wasn't expecting that and was pleased. "Why, sure! But it'll take more than just a few minutes if you're wanting what I'm wanting."

"All I want this evening is information."

She blinked. "What?"

Longarm decided that maybe Dolly wasn't a good person to confide in yet, so he said, "I'll be back another time."

"When?"

"I don't know."

She was confused, and it showed by her expression. "Well, don't wait too long, handsome. I've got plenty of choices around here."

"I'm sure you do," he said, paying his tab and tipping her generously before he left.

Longarm figured that by tomorrow everyone in Buffalo Falls would somehow know that he was a federal marshal sent from Denver. That being the case, he needed to circulate in the saloons tonight where whiskey and beer loosened tongues and clouded judgment.

So he headed over to the nearest saloon, called the Big Buck, and went inside. He was hoping that he wouldn't see either Wade Stoneman or Casey, but he immediately saw that Casey was sitting at a table playing poker. It was impossible to miss the white streak in the man's beard and Addie's description was very complete.

Longarm went to the bar and ordered a beer. "Looks like there's a pretty good poker game going on over there," he said.

"Yeah. Casey is winning tonight, so there won't be any bodies to bury come morning."

Longarm pretended to be shocked. "Which one is he?"

"The fella with all the chips as well as an even bigger chip on his shoulder. Stranger, you don't want to get into that game."

"Probably not," Longarm said. "I'm just here for a drink and maybe a little friendly conversation."

"You're new to Buffalo Falls?"

"I am. Thinking about buying a ranch."

"Think twice," the bartender whispered. "And when you learn a little more about things in this neck of the woods, you'll want to move on."

"Is that right?"

The bartender looked around and pretended to wipe a spill. "Don't tell anyone I said that, but this isn't the healthiest place in Wyoming these days. And if I wasn't part owner of this saloon, I'd be long gone."

"Why?"

"I can't say any more," the bartender whispered as a couple of cowboys entered the saloon and called for whiskey. "But just keep your wallet out of sight and your ears wide open. You'll find out what's up soon enough."

"Thanks for the advice," Longarm said, turning his full attention to Casey and the game of poker that he meant to join just as soon as a chair emptied.

A man could tell a lot about another man playing poker against him. He could tell if he was a bluffer or a foolish risk taker. If he was overly confident or reckless. Casey didn't look overconfident or reckless and from the way he wore his gun, he looked like a gunfighter to Longarm.

Why Addie's father had ever hired him in the first place was the biggest mystery of all, and one that Longarm intended to solve before this night was over.

Chapter 11

"Damn you, Casey, you're dealin' from the bottom of the deck again!" one of the poker players at the table shouted as he came to his feet and made a stab for his gun.

What happened next took less than a second. While the man was making his play, Casey's right hand appeared with a bowie knife whose huge blade was a silver blur as it slashed the loser's neck wide open, almost decapitating him. Blood burst like a fountain from the man's throat to spray across the poker table, chips, and cards a moment before he fell with his head barely attached to his shoulders.

The killing was so swift, brutal, and shocking that no one in the saloon moved or even took a breath. The dead man flopped around on the sawdust floor for a moment or two, and then was still.

Longarm watched Casey wipe his blade clean on another man's sleeve and then say as casually as if he were commenting on the weather, "He was wrong about me dealin' from the bottom of the deck. Did anybody else at this table see me cheating?"

The three surviving players were pale as ghosts and they couldn't shake their heads hard or fast enough.

"Of course you didn't," Casey said with a smile. "Bartender, come get this carrion out of here!"

"Yes sir, Marshal Casey!"

It was Longarm's turn to be shocked. Casey was the town's new *marshal*?

Longarm had been thinking about getting into the card game and somehow trying to provoke Casey or maybe even befriending him. Anything that would get the man to open up or reveal his true self. But now that wasn't going to be necessary. By his swift, brutal knife work, Casey had shown his true nature, and it was that of a cold-blooded killer with lightning-fast hands.

Longarm laid some money on the bar's top and went outside to clear his head. It wasn't that he hadn't seen men decapitated or nearly so before, because he had during the Civil War. Yet the cool and casual way that Casey had acted told Longarm that the man was totally without conscience. And how had he suddenly become the town's marshal? How could that be possible?

"Wade Stoneman," Longarm said, answering his own question. "Being the mayor of this town, he'd simply have recommended Casey for the job and that would have been more than enough to get him hired."

Longarm checked the time on his railroad pocket watch, the one whose chain was attached to a hideout derringer. It was almost ten o'clock, and it would take him about an hour to get back to the Lazy H Ranch, where Addie was waiting.

"I'll have another beer at a different saloon," he said

aloud. "I need to find out what I can before I call it a night."

The Red Garter Saloon was smaller, but friendlier than the Big Buck Saloon, where Longarm had just seen town Marshal Casey slash a man's throat. There was a piano player plinking out a tune on the east wall, and Longarm judged most of the customers to be town folks.

"What'll you have, stranger?" the bartender asked.

"A whiskey."

"You got it."

Longarm saw that there were no card games going on and that most of the men here were just drinking and talking among themselves. Some of them gave him a thorough appraisal when they didn't think he was noticing, and most of them seemed like solid citizens and businessmen. The only one he recognized was young Rollie Reed, the saddle maker.

Reed nodded to Longarm and started to come over and join him, but Longarm shook his head slightly. Taking the sign, Reed veered off and began talking to someone else as if he hadn't even seen Longarm.

"How is the cattle business around here?" Longarm asked, sidling over to a bowlegged man in his late sixties wearing spurs and a soiled vest. The man was too old and bent to be a working cowboy, and Longarm pegged him for a small-time cattle rancher.

"You askin' me?"

"That's right. My name is Long."

The cattleman was a lot shorter, but stocky and weathered by years in the saddle and the sun. "My name is Jed Dodson," the man said, extending a hand so rough and calloused it felt like rawhide. "And you are well named being as tall as you are. Why, you're as long as a grizzly's guts."

"My whole family was tall."

"Mine was short, like me. Why, my pa was so short he couldn't see over the top of a swaybacked burro, and my mother, bless her departed soul, she wasn't ankle-high to a June bug."

"Well," Longarm said, chuckling, "tall or short . . . it doesn't matter that much. It's what's on the inside of a man that counts."

"Amen to that! My folks were short but, Lord, were they hard workers. Both of 'em always kept as busy as one-armed monkeys at a flea farm."

Longarm burst out laughing. "Mister, you've got a colorful way of putting things."

"Well, anyone in Buffalo Falls will tell you that I talk way too much and think way too little. But I'm no braggart, and I'll readily admit that most of my life I've known times harder than a banker's heart."

"I'm in town looking for a ranch to buy," Longarm said, deciding that this man could shoot the breeze for hours and tell him nothing useful. "Or maybe just a business."

Dodson studied Longarm for a moment and then said, "Mister, either you're a cow man or you ain't. You can't just be on the fence about ranchin', Mr. Long. Remember that the fella that straddles the fence doesn't get nothin' but sore balls. Have you owned a ranch before?"

Longarm knew better than to lie because, if he did, Dodson would start talking cattle, prices, and grass and it would soon become apparent to the man that Longarm didn't know much at all about cattle ranching. So instead of lying, Longarm said, "Well, no. I just always thought it would be good way to live."

"Shee-it!" Dodson snorted, chuckling to himself. "Going into the cattle business is like droppin' your pants and tellin' the world to have their way with your asshole."

Longarm took a sip of his whiskey, deciding that he had probably picked the wrong man to talk to. When he looked over at Rollie Reed, the saddle maker was watching and trying not to burst into laughter.

"So," Longarm said, "ranching is that bad, huh?"

"Yep. I've been ranchin' for forty years and I'm still poorer than a toothless coyote. Why, during the worst of last winter, my cattle got so thin I had to wrap them in cowhide to keep 'em from fallin' apart. I could have made more money driving a stagecoach or workin' for the railroad. Any damn thing would have been more profitable."

"If you feel that way about ranching, then why don't you sell out and try something new?"

"'Cause I'm a cattleman and I am too dumb and too stubborn to quit." He smiled and finished his whiskey. "And besides that, I am way too mean and contrary to work for another yappy old sonofabitch like myself."

Dodson began to clear his throat.

"Are you all right?" Longarm asked with concern.

"Just real thirsty, I guess."

Longarm knew he'd been had. "In that case, old-timer, I'd better buy you a fresh drink."

"That'd be mighty neighborly of you. But I'll have to warn you that I won't buy you one back. People around here will tell you that I'm so stingy, I'd skin a flea for its hide and tallow."

"Don't worry about it, Jed. Just drink up and tell me about Buffalo Falls."

Jed Dodson seemed more than happy to do that. "What you want to know?"

"I heard that it's a nice town."

"Used to be," Dodson said, his smile dying. "Before a certain someone arrived."

"That right?"

Dodson studied Longarm a moment, then lowered his voice and said, "Why don't you bring a bottle over to that far table where we can talk in private."

Longarm decided that this might be time well spent after all. "Sure thing."

He paid for a bottle and made sure that he got the cork, because he'd take most of it back to the Lazy H tonight.

"You say you heard this is a fine town, huh?" Dodson asked at the table.

"That's what I'd heard," Longarm told the man.

"Well, if I was you, I'd keep lookin' for another town," Dodson told him in a low voice as he helped himself to Longarm's bottle. "'Cause you see, this town is cursed right now by a man named Wade Stoneman. *Mayor* Wade Stoneman. Him and his hired guns are going to own everything hereabouts lock, stock, and barrel. They're halfway to doin' it right now and any ranch you could buy wouldn't be worth spit, or Stoneman would already either own it or want to own it and both are the same thing."

"Does he want your ranch, Jed?"

"Damn right he does! And right now I'm feeling about as helpless as a cow in quicksand. But I'm stubborn like I told you and I'm hanging on and hopin' that

100

someone will kill Stoneman and his men will just go away."

"What about the marshal of Buffalo Falls?" Longarm asked, fishing for information. "Can't he help you?"

"Marshal Casey and Mayor Wade Stoneman get along like two shoats in a pigpen! Why, they're thicker'n feathers in a pillow!"

"I see."

"No," Dodson said, "I doubt that you do. But you will if you're dumb enough not to take my advice and light out of this town first thing in the morning."

Longarm watched Dodson toss down another shot and then he refilled the glass for the rancher. "Listen, Jed. Are you sober?"

"Sober enough."

"Can you keep a secret?"

"Hell, yes!"

Longarm lowered his voice so that they could not possibly be overheard. "Well, I'm a United States marshal and I was sent here from Denver to put a noose around Wade Stoneman's neck, and it looks like Marshal Casey is also going to dance on a rope."

Dodson's jaw sagged. "You're a federal marshal?"

"Shhh! Not so loud. People are going to find out about me soon enough, but I'm here tonight to try to learn as much as I can about Stoneman and Casey."

"What do you want to know? The mayor is so crooked he has to screw on his socks."

"Mr. Hudson, who owns the Lazy H Ranch, is dead. Addie and I found him shot behind his house."

Jed Dodson had been about to say something, but now he clamped his mouth shut and just stared into nothingness with tears filling his eyes. Finally, he choked out,

"Hank and I was friends for a lot of years. He was one of the best men I ever knew and there was many a time we helped one another out. We was close enough that we wouldn't even have minded usin' the same toothpick."

"I'm sorry to have to tell you this."

"Me, too," Dodson said with a sad shake of his head and a sleeve across his leaking eyes. Then his jaw clenched and he slammed a fist down on the table hard enough to make the bottle dance. "You just tell me who you think punched Hank's ticket and I'll fill the bastard with so many bullet holes he wouldn't even float in brine!"

"I don't know who killed him," Longarm said, not wanting this hot-blooded old cattleman to go off the deep end and get himself killed.

"Did Casey take all the slack out of Hank's rope!"

"I don't know. Maybe, but maybe not."

Dodson started to climb unsteadily to his feet. "I'll bet it was that sonofabitchin' Marshal Casey! I'll find him and kill him right now!"

"Jed, settle down! Less than thirty minutes ago, Casey nearly cut off a man's head with his bowie knife in the Big Buck Saloon!"

"Well, then, that's all the more reason to make him deader than a beaver hat!"

Everyone in the saloon had stopped talking and was staring. Longarm grabbed Dodson as the rancher struggled to unholster his gun and reel away. When Dodson batted his hand aside, Longarm could see that there was only one thing that he could do and that was to snatch the bottle of whiskey off their table and bust it across the back of Jed Dodson's thick skull.

The bartender hurried over and said, "Damn, mister, you really hit old Jed a lick! You might have killed him."

"Nope," Longarm assured him. "I just saved Jed's life. Help me drag him outside."

"Are you his friend?"

"I guess I am now whether I wanted to be or not."

"Jed is well liked in Buffalo Falls, but he keeps to himself. He had a wife once, but she died a long time ago."

"Any kids at his ranch?"

"No, he lives alone. He drove his boy crazy and so he went away and never came back."

"He's a talker all right," Longarm said. "Now help me get him outside to his horse."

They got Dodson on the boardwalk, and Longarm said, "Do you see Jed's horse tied up close around here?"

"Yeah, that good-looking gray belongs to Jed."

"Will you help me hoist him up into the saddle?"

"I guess." The bartender shook his head. "Jed won't stay up there because he's too drunk. Sober, he could ride a tornado. But he's in no shape to ride tonight. You really busted him hard."

Longarm knew this was true. "I know that, but at least he'll be alive tomorrow morning. And if he falls, I'll tie him down across his saddle."

"Listen," the bartender said, "I don't know who you are or why you're doing this, but I'm afraid that we all heard what old Jed yelled about Marshal Casey and Mr. Stoneman. When Jed sobers up, you better tell him to keep away from here for a while. A long damned while."

"I'll keep him out of town for the next few days even if I have to hogtie him. Where does Jed live?"

"About three miles out. Just south of the Lazy H. You know—"

"I can find it," Longarm interrupted as they heaved Jed up into the saddle, then held him there a minute. It wasn't a second before Jed started to lean and then fall. Grabbing the cattleman, Longarm said, "You were right about him pitching over. I'll tie him down across his saddle with his own rope."

"Best you do that," the bartender agreed. "People around here like old Jed. Be a shame if he fell and broke his neck. Be a shame, too, if he gets killed for shootin' off his mouth about Mayor Stoneman or Marshal Casey."

"I'll keep that from happening," Longarm promised.

"Who are you?" the bartender asked.

"Doesn't matter."

"It will to Mayor Stoneman and Marshal Casey. They'll hear about you helpin' Jed out of town and they'll be wanting to know who you are and why you did it."

Longarm was lashing the old cattleman across his saddle. The back of Jed's skull was bleeding and Longarm felt bad about having to really hurt him. But he knew that he had just saved the cattleman's life.

Chapter 12

On the way out of town, Longarm decided that the scalp wound he'd inflicted upon Jed Dodson probably needed suturing and that Addie was just the gal to do it. So he took the old rancher to the Lazy H, arriving there just before midnight. By that time, Jed Dodson was coming around and he was as mad as a teased rattlesnake.

"Damn you, Long! Get me down from this horse!" he yelled over and over. "Get me down and I'm gonna rip your ears off and feed 'em to my chickens!"

Longarm pulled up in front of the Hudson ranch house, which was lit up. Addie came rushing out onto the porch. "Custis, what have you done to poor old Jed!"

Longarm dismounted. "I had to waste a half bottle of whiskey that I busted over his granite skull."

"But . . . but why?"

"I'll tell you later," Longarm said. "Right now, let's get him down and inside. He's gonna need some stitching up and settling down."

Jed Dodson's legs had fallen asleep while he was draped over the back of his gray horse and all the blood had gone to his brain, so that when he was pulled off the

105

horse, instead of attacking Longarm, he fell over and passed out cold.

"That's a break," Longarm said, picking the man up under the arms and dragging him inside. "It'll make stitching up his head a whole lot easier and more pleasant."

"Bring him right in here," Addie instructed as she led the way into her kitchen. "And put him on the table. I'll get a needle and sutures. Why'd you have to hit him so damned hard?"

"He's a tough man to stop when he gets on the prod," Longarm said. "And I made the mistake of telling him that your father was murdered and I was pretty certain that Stoneman and Casey had their hands in it. When I told him that, Jed sorta went off the deep end and was determined to get himself killed."

"I see."

Addie handed Longarm a lamp and said, "Hold it close to his head so that I can cut off a little of this hair and then suture him up."

"I talked to Rollie Reed in town."

She looked up. "I'm glad. You can trust Rollie. He's a fine man and honest as the day is long."

"He said to tell you hello and he seemed glad that you finally came back . . . at least he did until he learned that I was staying here with you."

Addie had a pair of scissors and she was carefully cutting away the bloody, matted hair around the wound. "I think Rollie has always liked me."

"I'd say he feels a whole lot stronger about you than that. Rollie was sorry to hear about your father, and he told me that he'd do anything that he could to help take down Stoneman and Casey."

"That doesn't surprise me," Addie said. "And Rollie is capable with guns. He's not as good a shot as I am with a rifle, but he's much better than me with a pistol."

"I'll keep that in mind."

"Did you meet anyone else?"

"Dolly."

Addie almost smiled. "I'll bet that she was excited about meeting you."

"She . . . well," Longarm said, trying to put proper words to it. "She's uncommonly bold."

"That's a huge understatement. Dolly is pretty, but she sure goes through the men."

"So I gathered."

Addie's fingers were long and supple. Longarm watched while she did a fine job of quickly suturing up the laceration. "Almost done," Addie said. "Custis, what are we going to do with Jed when he wakes up wanting to kill you?"

"I think I better be out of his sight," Longarm answered. "Why don't you see if you can settle him down? If he still wants to go after Stoneman or Casey, we've got to convince him to back off or he'll be killed for certain. As it is, I'm afraid that word will get back to those two that old Jed is on the warpath and after their scalps."

"Jed needs to stay with us for his own protection."

Longarm frowned. "Do you really think that Stoneman or Casey would decide to kill him?"

"I'm sure of it," Addie replied. "They'd kill Jed in a minute, and then they'd forge his signature to some paper that said he'd sold his ranch to Wade Stoneman."

"And that would fly in Buffalo Falls?" Longarm asked with amazement.

"Sure. You can bet that Stoneman has the local judge deep in his pocket. He'd make the ruling and Jed's ranch would become another of Stoneman's properties."

Longarm shook his head in amazement. "That man has to be stopped."

"I know."

Longarm thought about it for a few minutes. "Maybe I can lure Casey or some of Stoneman's men to Jed's ranch. Set a trap for them."

"What are you talking about?" Addie asked, looking up with concern.

Longarm was thinking hard. "Well, I'll take Jed's gray horse back to his ranch and I'll tie the animal up in front of his house. If Casey or some of Stoneman's gunnies come to do Jed in, then I'll be there waiting to either kill or arrest them."

"If they don't kill you first! Custis, I think that's a terrible idea."

"I don't," Longarm replied. "It's a good way to get the ball rolling, and it won't be the first time I've laid a trap for killers."

"Are you sure you want to do that?"

"Hell, yes!" Longarm said. "I didn't plan it this way, but it'll work out for the best. If I'm lucky, Stoneman himself will come riding up to Jed Dodson's place with every intention of killing the old fart."

"But don't you understand that he'd have men with him? Seasoned gunfighters! How are you going to stand up against them?"

Longarm went over to the corner of the kitchen where he'd placed the big and finely crafted shotgun he'd bought in Cheyenne. "This is my edge, Addie. If I open up with both barrels, it won't matter how many men are standing in front of me."

"You can't go alone."

"I have to," Longarm insisted. "You need to keep Jed right here out of harm's way."

"He won't stand for that and neither will I." Addie finished with the scalp wound and put her sutures and medicine bag away. "Early in the morning, we'll all ride over to Jed's ranch house. We'll lay a trap and wait to see if trouble comes calling."

Longarm wanted to go to Dodson's ranch alone, but he could see that Addie wouldn't stand for that, and he knew that Jed would go crazy when he came around and learned what was going on. As hotheaded as the old cattleman was, he might just decide to come busting over to his ranch and mess up all of Longarm's plans.

"All right," Longarm reluctantly agreed. "To be honest, I could use some extra guns if Stoneman sends a bunch of gunnies."

"Sure you could." Addie smiled. "Let's get that old fella into bed. I expect he'll sleep until we're ready to go in the morning."

Longarm and Addie got Jed taken care of, and then they went to bed . . . but not to sleep. Addie began kissing him passionately, and soon Longarm was helping her tear off her clothes as well as his own.

He mounted Addie in her own bed, and they made lusty, passionate love as if there was not going to be a tomorrow. Addie started out on the bottom, but was soon on top and riding Longarm for all she was worth. At last, she let out a groan, and then Longarm slammed his seed up into her until he was fully emptied.

They toppled over and lay panting in the moonlight that slanted through Addie's window, each of them wondering what this coming day would bring and if Stoneman would send men with orders to shoot first and ask questions later.

After a while, Addie fell asleep, but Longarm was restless so he got up and quietly dressed. He checked his pocket watch and saw that it was two in the morning. Lighting a cigar, he went outside to sit on Addie's front porch and watch the moon and the stars. Sometime early that cold morning, he saw a shooting star, and Longarm took that as a good omen. Then he went inside and made a pot of strong black coffee.

"Custis?"

Longarm was stretched out on Addie's couch and he must have fallen asleep, because Addie was dressed and the sun was just coming up in the east.

"What time is it?" Longarm asked

"Almost six o'clock," she said. "I'm cooking breakfast and Jed is awake and feeling mighty grouchy. He wants to leave for his home, but I told him about how you wanted to set a trap and that we were going over to his ranch early this morning together."

Longarm knuckled the sleep out of his eyes. "Coffee sounds good," he said. "I made a pot early this morning and I thought it would keep me awake, but I still dozed off."

"Come and have some breakfast," Addie said. "And then you and Jed can get the horses ready to ride while I take care of a few last-minute things."

She started to turn away, but Longarm grabbed her wrist. "Addie, I can understand how Jed would feel mad at me and want to leave for his ranch, but I still think that you should wait here until this is over."

"Not a chance, so let's drop the subject. I've loaded my Winchester and I'm almost ready to leave," she said. "Don't you be talking any more foolishness. If Stoneman sends his troops over to Dodson's place, you're going to need me . . . and don't try to tell me that that shotgun will give you an advantage over a bunch of gunmen."

Longarm ran his fingers through his hair and yawned. "I never said anything about an advantage."

Jed Dodson stumbled into the room and glared at Longarm. "You big sonofabitch! You like to broke my skull last night."

"That's a whole lot better than getting yourself shot to death," Longarm answered.

Jed didn't seem to agree. "Marshal, if it weren't for the fact that you're trying to help Addie, I'd knock your ears down so far they'd look like little wings!"

"Take it easy, Jed. If Stoneman and his men come to kill you later today, you're going to have your chance to spill plenty of fresh blood . . . and it won't be mine."

Jed glared at Longarm and shouted, "The worst part of what you did last night was to waste half a bottle of good whiskey!"

"We'll have more after we take care of business," Longarm promised.

Addie frowned and said, "Boys, it's way too early in the morning for this and we're facing too much trouble to fight among ourselves. So come on into the kitchen and have coffee and breakfast. Then let's not waste any more time before we get riding."

"Suits me," Longarm said, feeling grumpy.

"Me, too, I guess," Jed groused as he strapped on his

gun. "But the inside of my old head feels like it's got two hungry badgers fightin' over what's left of my scrambled brains."

"You'll feel much better after you've had something to eat," Addie told him.

"I'd rather have the rest of that wasted whiskey."

But Longarm shook his head. "Jed, we're trying to save your ranch and I'll be damned if we need you drunk when trouble comes calling."

Jed could see the wisdom of Longarm's words, and he nodded reluctantly. "All right. Let's eat and then ride. But Stoneman better come or at least send some of his boys to my place, or I'm gonna be damned disappointed and unhappy."

Longarm almost smiled. Jed Dodson was a real pistol, that was for certain, and when it came time for a fight, if nothing else, the old man would be plenty game.

Chapter 13

"There it is," Jed told them as they topped a low rise and looked down toward his ranch. "That's my home sweet home. And out there by those trees behind the place is where my Rebecca is lyin' in wait for me. I put her up a good iron cross and painted it white like the little picket fence surrounding her. Can you see it?"

"I see it," Longarm said. "It's a nice place to lie in rest and in wait for you, Jed."

"Rebecca was the finest woman ever walked this land," Jed told them, his eyes faraway and dreamy. "She died one January when the temperature was forty below zero and the ice on the water tanks was a foot deep. I had to store her in the barn for two months until the weather warmed a mite. I used to go out and talk to her every night. 'Course, she was frozen and she even had a smile on her sweet face all that time. You know, I was almost sad when we got a spring thaw and I had to put her in the ground. But I still visit her every day."

"I remember your wife very well," Addie said. "She was a wonderful woman, kind, intelligent, and strong."

"She was all of that and more," Jed replied, his

voice hoarse now. "And I sure miss her. I'm glad that you remembered her so fondly, Addie. She always said that you were the daughter that she wished we'd had together. She thought of you that way . . . and so do I."

Longarm glanced at Addie, and he could see that she was so moved that she couldn't speak.

"It's a nice place," he said, eyes running over the ranch. "It's a real nice little ranch."

"I could never leave it," Jed told them. "Never get far from Rebecca or the ranch. We built it together. My son, he didn't want to live way out here. Wanted to go to the city and be more'n a cattleman. I never could understand that, but he's doing real well. Got a wife and two kids. I go to visit and they come up here to see me and Rebecca every summer. I've had a good life, but I sure do miss my girl."

Longarm studied the ranch house, barns, and corrals. It was clear that Jed Dodson's spread was considerably poorer than Addie's Lazy H, but any cowboy would have thought it a fine place to spend his final years. There were two windmills pumping water into two big stock tanks, and both the house and the barn were made from rough-hewn logs. The corrals were well built, and the whole place had a nice, homey look to it that made it easy to understand why Wade Stoneman would want the property.

"My wells are only thirty feet deep and they're pullin' up some of the sweetest water you ever tasted on this side of the Rocky Mountains," Jed told them.

"How much land do you own?" Longarm asked.

"It's a small spread, but big enough to support a family . . . if I had one anymore." Jed stood up in his stirrups to stretch his legs, and he rolled a smoke and lit it in the cup of his calloused hands. "I own two thousand, six hundred acres, but about half of my land is rocky mountain or in a steep canyon making it unfit for feedin' cattle. Still, with all the sweet water I've got, you can run about two hundred head of cattle in a good year with summer rains to bring up the tall grass."

"It's a handsome ranch," Longarm said admiringly after they'd sat and looked over the ranch for a few minutes. "Why don't we get down there and tie your gray horse up in front of the house while Addie and I hide our horses in that barn."

Jed Dodson was starting to feel better and he finished his smoke, ground it out on his saddle horn, and put the remains of it in his shirt pocket. Then he gathered his reins and said, "Yes, sir, this is a fine morning. Cold and clear. I sent my cattle to market last month and did pretty well on 'em."

Addie looked over at him. "I don't expect you put your cattle money in Stoneman's Buffalo Falls bank."

"Hell, no! I put half in the bank in Cheyenne and the other half I hid so nobody could find it."

"Good idea," Longarm said as they rode down to the ranch house.

As planned, Addie and Longarm put their horses in the barn, leaving them saddled and bridled just in case things didn't go as expected and they needed to make a hard, fast run for it.

When they came up to the house, Jed came out of the kitchen and said, "I'm brewin' more coffee. It'll only be a little while. Gonna get the stove fired up because it's chilly in here."

"Take your time," Longarm answered, thinking that a

good fire in the stove would put smoke out the chimney and tell anyone coming that Jed was up and going about his daily chores.

"How long do you think it might be before Casey or Stoneman and his boys make an appearance?" Addie asked.

Longarm shrugged. "Could be soon, might never happen. I don't know. But my guess is that, if they're going to come for Jed, they'll do it first thing this morning."

"I hope so," Addie nervously replied. "If we're going to have a fight, the sooner the better."

"My sentiments exactly," Longarm told her. "As it is, we'll just have to keep inside and out of sight. Jed can go outdoors, but he'll have to keep a sharp eye out for someone with a high-powered rifle and scope. You never can tell, they might just send one man . . . someone like Casey . . . to ambush him from long distance."

Addie turned toward the kitchen. "Did you hear that, Jed! Custis says that when you go out you'll have to watch for an ambusher."

"I heard him," Jed hollered back at them. "And I expect he's right. Rather than ride up here and maybe take a chance that I'd kill one or two, they're such cowards that they would try to pick me off from the trees out back or maybe from that ridge we rode down off."

Longarm yawned, and that caused Addie to do the same. She smiled and said, "We didn't get much sleep last night."

"No, but I hope you're not regretting it."

"I'm not if you're not," she told him. "Still and all, I wouldn't mind sleeping awhile. I'm so tired this morning that I'm afraid that I might not be able to shoot straight."

"I'm a little strung out myself," Longarm confessed. "Jed is the only one who got a good night's sleep last night."

"Maybe he'll let us take a long nap while he watches over things," Addie suggested.

She went into the kitchen where Jed was making coffee, and when she came out she said, "Jed says for us to go into his bedroom and sleep awhile."

"Does he know that he'll have to be very careful and keep a sharp lookout if he goes outside?"

"He does," Addie said. "I told him again that you were concerned about an ambusher, and he agreed to be watchful for trouble and wake us up if he even suspected riders were coming from Buffalo Falls."

"Good enough," Longarm said. "Let's get some shut-eye."

"Are you sure that's *all* that you want?" Addie asked with knowing smile. "I mean, can I really trust you to lie down beside me and go to sleep?"

"You can this morning," Longarm told her, feeling his eyes burn.

So they went into the bedroom and lay down on Jed's mattress and went to sleep.

Longarm awoke to the sound of a high-powered rifle. Maybe one of those big buffalo rifles that could shoot accurately from several hundred yards. Anyway, it wasn't a Winchester. Longarm knew that the moment its sound rolled over the log ranch house.

"Addie!" he shouted at the woman sleeping beside him. "Wake up!"

She was slower coming out of sleep than Longarm, and he gave her such a shove that she rolled off the bed and hit the floor. "Ouch!"

Longarm had taken his boots and gunbelt off, but now he pulled them on and hurried out of the bedroom into the front room. The front door was closed and the fire in the stove was really putting out the heat. "Jed!"

No reply.

Longarm knew then that the old rancher had gone outside, probably to his barn to feed and water their saddled horses. However, when Longarm glanced out into the yard, his heart sank to his feet.

Jed had been shot. There was blood on his coat and he was lying facedown with a spilled bucket of oats in his outstretched hand. He wasn't moving, but Longarm thought he saw one of the old man's fingers twitch. It was impossible to tell if he was fatally wounded.

"Jed!" Addie called, stumbling out of the bedroom still half asleep but coming awake fast.

Longarm grabbed Addie and pulled her down with him on the floor. She struggled. "Custis, we've got to help him! Jed may be bleeding to death!"

"We can't help him by getting ourselves ambushed like he just did," Longarm told her.

"But what are we going to do!" Addie cried, still trying to break out of Longarm's grasp and run outside to the old cattleman's aid.

"We've got to let whoever did that come in closer," Longarm told her. "There may be one ambusher. There may also be half a dozen gunmen and right now they're waiting to see if anyone else is here besides Jed."

"But—"

"Addie," Longarm said, trying to make her understand, "if you go out into that yard, one of two things is going to happen and both will be bad. Either they'll shoot you like they shot Jed, or they'll hightail it out of here for town and we'll never know just who shot Jed."

"How long will we have to wait like this!"

Addie was nearly sobbing, and Longarm knew that she desperately wanted to go to Jed Dobson's side and see if she could help him. And Longarm wanted that almost as much, but he knew better than to move until the ambusher and whoever he was riding with came into the yard. Then Longarm and Addie would have a chance to take their revenge.

"Steady, Addie! You've got to hold tight!" Longarm hissed. "Crawl over there and get your rifle. You can't let yourself be seen through the front window. I'll get the shotgun and when they ride into the yard to make sure that Jed is finished, that's when we'll open up on them with all we've got."

Addie swallowed hard and bit her lip. "But what if they just ride away now and not come in close? If they did that while poor old Jed bled to death as we watched, I'd never forgive myself."

"They won't do that," Longarm told her. "Trust me on this one. They'll have to make sure the old man is dead, and they probably even know about his hidden cattle money. No, Addie, they'll come in and when they dismount, we open fire."

"Do you know how many?"

"I'm not sure, but I bet Casey is one of them."

"You didn't think it's Wade Stoneman?"

"No," Longarm said, "he's too smart to do his dirty work."

"Dammit!"

"I know," Longarm said. "But don't worry. We'll get him sooner or later."

"Let's just try to come out of this alive and then see if I can help Jed."

"Addie, it sure would be good to take one of them alive. I could force him to testify in Cheyenne against Wade Stoneman. Make him tell a judge that he was sent by Wade to kill old Jed. Once he confessed, I could get a warrant for Stoneman's arrest and bring him down."

"Does that mean you're going to try to wing one of them?"

"No," Longarm answered. "We're too badly outnumbered for that. I'm going to shoot to kill. But maybe one of them will still be alive when the smoke clears."

Longarm had the shotgun ready and he was packing two pistols. He eased up beside the front window and raised his head just slightly to see five riders coming off the ridge. One of them was Casey. Longarm recognized the man from the way his hat was curled down on one side and up on the other.

"Addie," he said, "there are five of them riding off the ridge. Casey is in the middle of the bunch and he's got a big rifle resting on the fork of his saddle. I'd bet anything that he was the man who just shot Jed."

"This is killing me not being able to go to help Jed. Custis, that poor old man may be bleeding out!"

"I know," Longarm told her. "But he could be alive and is just playing possum. And he might even have a gun in his hand waiting for Casey and the others to ride in close."

"I hope you're right!"

Longarm turned and gripped Addie by the shoulders.

"Listen to me," he whispered. "Those men aren't cowboys and they aren't farmers. They're hired gunmen. Professionals. We're going to need the element of surprise plus a little good luck. So if you can't do this, Addie, crawl back into the bedroom and be still because I can't worry about you when the shooting starts!"

Addie took a deep breath. "I'll be all right," she said, nodding her head up and down and making an obvious effort to get herself under control.

"Can I count on you?" Longarm asked, loosening his grip and staring into her eyes.

"You can count on me."

"To do as I tell you and not shoot until I do?"

"Yes!"

"All right," Longarm said, letting her go. "Just move over to the other side of the window, but stay down low. When it's time, I'll go through the door with this shotgun and open up on them with both barrels. After I do that, you shoot right through the window at anyone still moving other than myself. Don't get rattled and shoot me in the back by mistake, Addie."

"I won't."

"Fair enough," Longarm said, cocking back both hammers on the European eight-gauge shotgun and making sure that his Colt revolver was loose in its holster.

Longarm peeked over the windowsill and watched as Casey and the four gunmen rode into the yard looking mostly at the house, but also missing nothing in the yard.

When they were within fifteen yards of the prostrate Jed Dodson, Longarm moved away from the window to the door. He put his hand on the knob and turned it slowly, then opened it a crack. All five men

121

had dismounted and were staring at Dodson, who looked dead.

Longarm distinctly heard Casey say, "Roll the old bastard over. I want to see if I got him in the heart."

One of the gunmen stepped over to the body and reached down to turn Jed over onto his back. That's when the old rancher yanked his gun up and shot the gunman squarely in the face. Stoneman's hired gun reached up to cover his face and then toppled over backward. Longarm could tell that he was dead even before he struck the hard-packed dirt.

Longarm saw Casey and the other three men go for their guns, and that's when he jumped out on the front porch and squeezed off both barrels of the shotgun. The thunder was so loud and the recoil so powerful that it knocked him a step back into the doorway. A huge cloud of smoke billowed outward, and then Addie opened fire, her bullets smashing through the front window of Jed's log house.

Longarm dropped to one knee and drew his six-gun. The smoke was so thick from the twin blasts of the shotgun that it was a moment before he could see any targets. And when he could see, all of Wade Stoneman's gunfighters were down, but they weren't all dead.

Casey was alive and he was pulling his gun up to fire when Longarm fired two bullets at the man. His first bullet struck Casey in the shoulder, and his second hit the killer in the mouth, tearing off one side of his head.

Addie was still firing and she drilled one of the killers in the chest, and when he rolled, she shot him a second time just to make sure he was dead.

"Stop!" Longarm called. "Addie, hold your fire!"

Longarm jumped off the porch and ran over to Jed Dodson, who had collapsed in the dirt with fresh wounds, probably from Longarm's shotgun.

"Addie!"

"I'm coming!"

She was beside him in a moment holding her medical kit. She felt for a pulse in Jed's throat and, to Longarm's surprise, found one.

"He's alive, but barely," she said, tears in her eyes. "Let's get him in the house quick!"

Longarm started to grab and lift the old man, but something out of the corner of his eye caused him to twist around. One of the gunmen was still alive and he was trying to raise his pistol.

Needing a witness against Wade Stoneman, Longarm made a split-second decision and slashed his gun down on the man's head, knocking him unconscious.

"Hurry!" Addie cried. "Jed is bleeding badly!"

Longarm scooped up Jed Dodson and carried him back into the ranch house on the run. They laid him on the table just as they'd done last night when the rancher had needed sutures in his scalp. Addie went right to work on Dodson, but she was crying.

"I don't think he's going to make it!"

"Try, Addie! That's all you can do is try to save him."

Longarm rushed back outside and checked on the downed men one by one. The big Belgian shotgun had done a hideous piece of work on all of the men save for the one that Longarm had pistol-whipped. That man was still breathing.

After making sure that he was unarmed, Longarm gathered him up and dragged him into the house, then dumped him on the floor and went back to stand beside Addie.

Jed Dodson *was* dying, but the old man was still conscious. "Addie," Jed whispered, "did you and the marshal get all of them sonsabitches!"

"Yes. Don't try to talk. Save your strength."

"I'm finished," Jed whispered. "Addie, don't mourn me. I'll soon be meetin' your old man and we can swap lies in heaven. I know it's my time to saddle a cloud and ride to the great beyond."

"Jed, I'm going to try and stop this bleeding and . . ."

The rancher rolled his head back and forth on his scarred kitchen table. "Get me pen and paper, Addie. I'm going to write my will. I want you to see that my boy gets my cattle sale money. Will you do that?"

"Of course! But . . ."

"Listen to me, girl!" Jed spat up blood and struggled for breath. When it came, he whispered, "Addie, I want you to have my ranch. It borders your own. I want you to have it and never let Stoneman get his meat hooks into it! Hear me?"

Longarm could see that the old man was floating in and out of consciousness. His breath was coming in spasms. There was blood all over the table and dripping onto the floor. It was incredible that Jed Dodson was still hanging on.

"Addie, bury me beside my missus! Will you do that?"

Addie was sobbing while Longarm found writing materials. "I'll do that," Addie promised.

Somehow, Jed Dodson scribbled out a hasty will, and then he whispered, "Aw, Addie, I'm seein' a sky of gold and pink and it's prettier than a rainbow, all . . . all waitin' for me to ride that cloud to the Promised Land. Addie!"

Before she could answer, the old cattleman was gone.

•

Chapter 14

"Is that young man still alive?" Addie asked after a few minutes of silence.

Longarm twisted around and looked at the gunman. "He was when I brought him in, but he's hurt bad."

Addie stroked Jed's cheek for a moment, and then she took a deep breath and said, "We'd better try to save that young man even if he does work for Wade Stoneman."

"If we can, then we've got a witness that will testify against Stoneman. Addie, that man could be the key to bringing Stoneman to trial. If you can save him, then do it."

They carried Jed Dodson into the parlor and laid him out on the floor. Then Longarm lifted the man he'd badly wounded up onto the table so that Addie could attend to him.

"Help me get him undressed," Addie ordered. "He has been hit by scattershot from his knees up to his neck. He's bleeding from about five places, but I won't know if he has any chance to live until I can do a full body examination."

127

Longarm used a knife to cut the man's bloody clothing away. When he got him stripped down to his underpants, he hesitated.

"I'm a doctor," Addie said. "He might have gotten shot in the groin. Take *everything* off."

Longarm stripped the bleeding man naked and stepped back to take his measure. He was young . . . probably in his early twenties . . . and he was tall, slender, and quite handsome. He had sandy brown hair and a strong chin. Longarm noted that the badly wounded man also had a lot of scars on his back, chest, and buttocks.

"He's been beaten relentlessly," Addie said, asking for a wet kitchen towel so she could wipe away the blood and see exactly how bad this man was shot. "I'd guess he was savagely whipped as a boy. Probably by a father or a relative. No kid should have had to endure such a beating."

"Doesn't excuse him for turning into a killer," Longarm told her.

"We don't know if he ever killed anyone or not," Addie countered. "He might have, but I don't see how we can be the judge of that. All I'm saying, Custis, is that this young man has had a very cruel upbringing."

Longarm took the bloody towel and wrung it out over the kitchen sink, then wet it again and gave it back to Addie. "How many lead pellets did he take from my eight-gauge?"

"At least five. Two in the legs, three in the body." Addie placed her finger over a bleeding hole just to the right of the man's belly button. "The worst is definitely this one. I'm afraid that it might have penetrated his stomach cavity, and it'll have to come out if he has any chance to live. If it's punctured his gut, he's already a

128

dead man. I won't know until I get it out and we see how he does during the next twenty-four hours."

"That long?"

"If he's still alive in twenty-four hours, he has a fighting chance," Addie said, digging into her medical bag for a pair of long-nosed forceps. "I'm just not sure that I can find the lead shot."

Longarm nodded with understanding. "A gut wound is fatal," he said. "I've seen a lot of them and no one who had a gut wound ever survived."

"It may have just missed his stomach and come to rest in his abdominal muscle," Addie said, wiping the wound clean. "These other wounds are obviously into muscle, and I can dig the lead out after we see to this one."

Longarm gazed down without sympathy at the young gunman. "Do you want me to hold him down on the table?"

"Yes," Addie said. "He might come awake due to the pain and start fighting me."

Longarm pinned the man's arms to his sides and watched as Addie doused the wound with some antiseptic that she had in a corked blue bottle. "I've got to get this out fast or he's going to bleed to death," Addie said more to herself than to Longarm.

Addie had long, supple fingers, and now she gripped the silver forceps and slipped them into the wound. She frowned with intense concentration, and Longarm could see that she had begun to sweat even though it wasn't all that warm in the kitchen.

Addie closed her eyes and said, "I was taught by a very good surgeon that these little pieces of lead go deep and the only way that you can possibly extract them out is to close your eyes and concentrate on feel."

"You can *feel* the lead shot?"

"I hope so," Addie told him. "I've never done one that is this deep. My thinking is that, if I feel my forceps close on something solid, it has to be the lead from your shotgun's blast."

"If he dies, it's nobody's fault but his own," Longarm told her. "But we sure could use his testimony."

Addie wasn't really listening because she was concentrating so hard. After several minutes, a very slight smile touched her lips and she whispered, "I think I've got it!"

"Well, pull it out and let's see."

Addie squeezed the forceps and slowly extracted a piece of twisted lead about the size of a flattened pea.

"You did it!" Longarm said, genuinely impressed. "Do you think that lead was inside his gut?"

"No," Addie replied, dropping the lead shot onto the table and leaning forward with relief. "It was embedded in muscle."

Addie found bandaging in her medical kit and stuffed some cotton in the hole, and then she went to work on the other less critical wounds. Longarm kept expecting the young killer to come awake and begin to thrash, but he never did.

"How hard did you hit him over the head with your gun?" Addie asked when she had examined and extracted shot from all five wounds and then closed them up with either sutures or bandages. "I am wasting my time if you scrambled his brain like you almost did poor Jed's."

"I just gave him a good, solid tap on the skull. If he doesn't make it, it won't be because of my pistol-whipping."

"I certainly hope not," she said, finishing her doctoring. "He's a handsome young man and if he lives, maybe he'll take this as a lesson and change his ways."

"Maybe," Longarm said, though he doubted it. "All I want is for this fella to live long enough to testify in Cheyenne against Wade Stoneman. If he does that, he can die or go to prison and live; it doesn't matter to me one way or the other."

"Well, *I* want him to live," Addie said with conviction. "I never had a patient that was shot as badly as this young man. I'm just glad that the pattern from that shotgun hit him low and not in the head. If it had, he'd have been killed on the spot."

"Just like Casey and the others," Longarm said, thinking about all the bodies outside that would need burying. "I told you when I bought that shotgun in Cheyenne that it would make all the difference if we got in a tight spot and were outnumbered."

Addie finished up her work on the unconscious young man and said, "Did you check this man's pockets to see if he had anything personal that would tell us his name or where he came from? If he dies, it would be nice to notify his next of kin. This man probably has a mother who loves him. It's the least we can do."

Longarm disagreed. "I haven't got time to notify the next of kin. Casey and three other gunmen are lying dead out there in Jed's ranch yard, and all of them deserved what they got after they ambushed old Jed. Besides, if I tried to contact all their next of kin, I'd never get to what really needs doing and that's bringing Stoneman down."

"I understand," Addie said patiently. "But . . . but, well, this young man might have been spared for a good purpose. Who are we to say that he couldn't turn over a new leaf and become a fine citizen?"

"I'm not saying he couldn't," Longarm replied, "but I am saying that a leopard doesn't change its spots and that if this young fella lives, don't you expect him to become a Bible-thumping solid citizen. That's just not being realistic."

I know, but he's such a handsome lad." Addie's fingers touched his pale cheek. "You know something? I'll bet he's broken a few hearts in his short life, and he might even have a sweetheart waiting somewhere. Check his pockets, Custis."

Longarm retrieved the man's bloody pants and shirt. He rummaged through his pockets, and danged if there wasn't a bloodstained but readable envelope and letter.

"It's addressed to a Mr. Joel Crawford in Cheyenne."

"So his name is Joel," Addie said, looking pleased. "Open up the letter inside," Addie urged, spreading a blanket over the man. "Let's find out who sent him that letter."

Longarm unfolded the letter, and damned if it wasn't from the man's sweetheart, a girl in Omaha, Nebraska, of all places.

"She says that she misses him a lot and that she wants to leave her parents' farm before Christmas so that they can be married. She says that she would love being his wife and living in Cheyenne, but thinks that she would rather live in California . . . if they could get the money to travel that far."

Addie grinned. "California, huh?"

"Yep," Longarm said, scanning through the letter. "His girlfriend doesn't say where she got the notion that California would be a good place to live, but she says that she'd live almost anywhere except Nebraska after they were married." Longarm tried to wipe away a spot of blood that was blotting out a few of the girl's words.

"Go on," Addie urged.

"There's a little part here too smeared with blood to read, but later on she says that she loves him and wants them to have a lot of children, mostly boys because they would all be tall and handsome like their father."

Tears sprang to Addie's eyes and she scrubbed them away. "Did she leave a return address so that we could contact her?"

"Nope. She just signed the letter Betsy."

"Too bad," Addie said, obviously disappointed. "If Joel Crawford dies, we will never know how to contact Betsy and tell her what happened to the young man she loves."

"That would be a mercy for Betsy," Longarm reckoned aloud. "Why would she want to know that her lover was gunned down by a lawman after he was in on something bad like he was?"

"I guess you've got a good point," Addie said, adjusting the blanket. "But I sure hope our Joel doesn't die."

"Yeah," Longarm agreed. "If you plan to practice medicine around here, it wouldn't be good if your first gunshot patient shipped out."

"That wasn't why I was hoping he'd make it," Addie told him with some exasperation.

"Maybe not," Longarm said, "but this fella would be a real good advertisement for your skills, if he makes it and testifies."

"I expect he probably would," Addie agreed. "We've got a lot of burying to do."

Longarm nodded. "I'll start digging a grave for Jed beside his wife Rebecca. But I'm not planting Casey

133

and those other three riddled bastards anywhere near Jed and his wife."

"We probably ought to take them into town and have the undertaker bury them, but I can't leave Joel in his critical condition."

"And I'm not going to do it either," Longarm said. "I'll plant Casey and his friends in shallow graves up on the ridge. If someone ever wants to claim the bodies, they can dig them up and do what they will. But I'm not going to any extra trouble."

"Let's get Jed buried properly and then we can take it from there," Addie suggested.

"Okay."

Longarm went out, and it took him an hour to catch the horses that Casey and his men had owned. He hid those animals out of sight in the barn. After that, he fed and watered them, and then he found a shovel and went to the little cemetery where Rebecca Dodson lay long buried.

"I'm bringing your husband back to you," Longarm said as he shoveled dirt. "We're gonna lay Jed down beside you just like he wanted. And for what it's worth, Mrs. Dodson, I hope you and Jed are already holdin' hands in heaven."

It was mid-afternoon before Longarm had finished all the burying. Five graves, four of them shallow and one deep, and with words from the Holy Bible said over that grave so that Jed was sent off properly.

After that, Longarm went into the house and washed the dirt off himself, and then he lay down to take a much-needed nap.

"Stand the watch, Addie. By now, Stoneman must be

134

wondering why his boys haven't returned to Buffalo Falls."

"Do you think he'll come out here to find out why they didn't return?"

"I sure as hell hope so," Longarm answered as he pulled the brim of his Stetson over his eyes and fell asleep almost instantly.

Chapter 15

"Custis!"

He awoke with a start. "What?"

Addie had her Winchester clenched in her fists. "There are some horsemen coming!"

Longarm swung his legs off the bed and struggled to shake off a long, deep sleep. He grabbed his six-gun and hurried into the living room still in his stockings. "Four of them. And damned if one of them isn't the big man himself, Wade Stoneman!"

Longarm had a little time, so he went back into the bedroom and pulled on his boots and then gathered his hat. He reloaded the eight-gauge shotgun and said, "Addie, just stay back out of sight and don't make a peep. If shooting starts, then you know how to use that Winchester and don't hesitate to do it, because Stoneman wouldn't dare let you live to tell how he and his men shot down a federal marshal."

"Do you think they'll do that?"

"When they learn what I've done, they might just try," Longarm said. "Then again, Stoneman knows that I won't back down or waver for an instant if the bullets start flying."

"Are you going to tell him about Joel Crawford still being alive and our plans to take him to see a judge in Cheyenne?"

"I'd best not," Longarm said after giving the question a moment's thought. "But I'm sure he'll figure out that's what I intend to do if he knows the kid has survived."

"Be careful!"

Longarm finished loading and cocking back both hammers on the shotgun. "You know I will be, and that this big gun almost evens the fighting odds."

Addie kissed him on the lips.

"What was that for?" he asked with surprise.

"For luck. If you die out there, I'm going to die, and I'd like to see us buried side by side like the Dodsons."

Longarm was touched by the sentiment. It was something that he hadn't expected to hear from a woman he still did not know all that well, and he didn't have any words to give her back, so he stepped outside onto the porch and waited for the riders.

Stoneman didn't recognize Longarm until he was less than fifty feet from the ranch house, and when he did he gaped, but then quickly recovered his composure and grinned.

"Well, as I live and breathe, if it isn't my old friend and student Marshal Custis Long!"

Longarm nodded. "I'm no student anymore, Wade. I wasn't when you left Denver."

"Yeah," Stoneman said, reining in his horse as the three men he'd brought did the same. "I can see that you've really filled out those boots. Are you still work-ing for Billy Vail?"

Longarm nodded. "I am."

How is old Billy? Probably fatter than a hog after a few years sitting behind a government desk."

"Billy is fine," Longarm said. "He sent me here."

Stoneman blinked. "Billy sent you?"

"That's right."

"Why? Did he think you missed your old friend and mentor?"

"I don't think that's the reason," Longarm answered. "Billy got word that you were doing some things that go against the law."

Stoneman feigned surprise and hurt. "I can't believe that Billy would think bad of me."

"He and a lot of other people in this neck of the woods think bad of you, Wade. From what I hear, you've managed to scare everyone into either selling out or making you emperor of Buffalo Falls, or else you've killed them off. Three city councilmen?"

Wade's smile died. He was a big and handsome man, but too much money and good food had put forty extra pounds on his frame and he looked older and dissipated. Under the brim of his Stetson, there was now silver in-stead of black hair. Yet when Longarm looked into Wade's black eyes, he saw a familiar unyielding intensity and resolve. And the same lack of compassion. Longarm had always thought that gazing into Wade Stoneman's eyes was like staring into the eyes of a mountain lion.

Wade turned away from Longarm for a moment and surveyed the ranch yard.

Longarm knew that he was looking for the men he'd

sent to kill Jed Dodson. "Wade, are you looking for something you might have lost?"

"No," Wade said, still not looking back at Longarm. "I was just thinking that this is a fine little ranch. A ranch I'd like to own. I think I'll buy it from Jed the next time I see him. Make him a fair offer and send him on his way to Cheyenne, where he can sit in a rocking chair and get regular visits from his son. How does that sound, Custis?"

"Sounds kind of like you've made up your mind to have this ranch no matter what Jed wants."

"Boss?"

It was one of Stoneman's hired guns, and he was looking as if he wanted to go for his gun.

"What?"

"You want me to ride around and maybe look in the barn?"

"No!" Stoneman lowered his voice and said to his men, "Let's all relax and sit tight for the moment."

His mounted gunmen nodded with understanding.

Now Stoneman turned back to study Longarm. "What in the hell are you doing here?"

"I made friends with Jed."

"You should be more careful choosing your friends, Custis. I hear that Jed was saying some unpleasant things about me in the saloon last night. I'm afraid that Jed has misjudged me and I wanted to sort of . . . well, clear the air with him today. Is he inside?"

"No," Longarm said.

"Then where is he?"

"Jed is around," Longarm answered. "I'll tell him that you came to make him another offer for this ranch, but don't expect him to sell."

"Why not? Every man has his price. Even you."

"I don't think so."

"Why don't I see if that is true or not?" Stoneman suggested. "How much money are you making by now working as a federal marshal?"

"Deputy marshal," Longarm corrected.

"Ah, you haven't advanced up the career ladder?" Stoneman made a face reflecting disappointment. "Too bad, but to be honest, I'm not really surprised. I know from firsthand experience that you are brave and resourceful, but I also remember you had little or no ambition."

"I've got ambition," Longarm countered. "I get real ambitious when it comes to arresting someone for murder."

Stoneman took a deep breath, and Longarm could see that he had really rankled the former lawman. "And are you here to arrest *me*?"

Longarm lifted the barrel of the huge shotgun so that it was pointed right at Stoneman. "Not yet. But if you or one of your men even drop your hands a little, there won't be any need to arrest you or them . . . because you'll be deader than cans of corned beef."

Stoneman was fearless and cunning. And he damned sure wasn't going to make a false move and get himself blown to pieces. "Now just settle down there, Custis! That's mighty hard talk for an old friend that saved your life more than once, as you seem to have forgotten."

"I haven't forgotten," Longarm told him. "And I also remember saving your life in Santa Fe when you tried to rape that little Mexican girl that had served us supper."

"Ah," Stoneman exclaimed, "you do remember a thing or two from our storied past."

"Most of those memories are bad, Wade."

Stoneman placed both of his big hands on his saddle horn. "So where exactly is Jed Dodson?"

"Like I said before, Jed is around."

Stoneman frowned and seemed to think hard for a few moments. Finally, curiosity got the better of him and he asked, "You haven't by any chance seen any of my riders today, have you?"

"What would they be doing on Jed's ranch?"

"Oh," Stoneman said, broad shoulders shrugging off the question. "Sometimes my cowboys tend to wander a mite."

"How many of them were there?" Longarm was almost starting to enjoy this cat-and-mouse game.

"Five."

"Hmmm," Longarm murmured. "That's a lot of men to lose. Are you sure you sent them over here?"

"I didn't send them anyplace," Stoneman countered. "But they might have been looking for cattle and ridden in this general direction. One of them was a top hand named Casey."

"And that would be the new town marshal? Is he one of your lost cowboys, Wade?"

Stoneman realized that he'd made his own trap and now he was angry. "Listen, Custis, don't even start to play games with me! If you have something to say, then say it now and let's get down to brass tacks. You know I'm not the kind of man that likes to put unpleasant things off until later."

"All right," Longarm agreed, deciding to lay his cards on the table. "I'm here to take you down, Wade. I can kill you right now, but I'd rather see you go to trial and then the gallows."

His face flushed with red anger. "That will *never* happen. You know it and so do I."

Longarm did know that Stoneman would never allow himself to hang. He'd go down fighting if cornered, and he was starting to feel a bit cornered right now even though he had three gunmen who looked tough and capable.

"I believe our conversation is over," Longarm said.

"Yeah, I think you're right about that. Will you be coming into Buffalo Falls anytime soon?"

"I probably will, Wade."

"Good! Then drop by my office at the bank and I'll pour you a glass of whiskey or a cup of Colombian coffee . . . whichever you prefer."

"I'll keep your invitation in mind."

"You know," Stoneman said, lifting his reins, "it doesn't have to be this way between old friends. I'll pay you double . . . no, triple . . . what you're earning as a marshal, and there would be bonuses that could make you wealthy."

"No, thanks."

"See, you have no ambition." Stoneman looked at his gunmen. "Custis Long is a formidable man . . . someone not to be taken lightly. But his problem was and still is that he is stupid and has no ambition."

Longarm had no intention of being insulted. "So long, Wade. I'll be seeing you again before long."

Stoneman started to rein his horse around, and then he paused and said, "Oh, by the way. I hear that Addie Hudson came back from Denver. She didn't by chance happen to come back with you, did she?"

"She might have."

He grinned. "Always the ladies' man, Custis. They always loved you the most and the best."

Stoneman stared at the ranch house. "She wouldn't just happen to be inside there, would she?"

"Why do you ask?"

"Just wondering. I like her ranch, too."

"I'll bet."

Stoneman laughed a cold, hard laugh. "I wouldn't mind owning the Lazy H, and I'd like it even better if Addie came with it."

"Dream on," Longarm said.

"Have you screwed her, Custis? I'll bet you have? Is she as juicy as she looks?"

Longarm raised the big double-barreled shotgun and pointed it right at Stoneman's grinning face. "You've got about two seconds to ride out of here before I blow you all over the yard."

"Ah, I hit a nerve. It tells me that you have bedded her! Well, good for you!"

Longarm started to squeeze the triggers, but a cry from the house stopped him cold. "Custis, no!"

Stoneman and his riders stared at Addie in the doorway with her Winchester.

"Well, doesn't this just make things even more interesting," Stoneman said, grinning from ear to ear. "What a stir this is going to cause among the ladies of Buffalo Falls."

"Git!" Longarm said. "Git while you can."

"This is just the beginning," Stoneman warned. "I'll be seeing you in *my* town one of these days real soon."

"Wade, you can count on it," Longarm promised the

big man before Stoneman jerked his horse around and galloped away.

"So what are we going to do now?" Addie asked after the riders were gone.

Longarm frowned. "Do you think that Crawford is going to make it?"

"I expect he will live. But we can't move him right away."

Longarm considered their dilemma for a moment. "All right," he decided. "We'll wait until it gets dark and then we'll take him to your place for a couple of days."

"And then what?"

"I haven't figured that out yet," he admitted. "I guess the main thing is that we get him to a judge in Cheyenne. After he gives sworn testimony against Wade, then I'll have grounds for an arrest warrant."

Addie thought about this for a few seconds, then said, "What about all those horses you hid in the barn?"

"We'll take them and hide them in your barn until I figure out what to do next. Addie, the important thing is to get Joel to Cheyenne alive so he can testify against Wade."

"And what if he refuses to do that?"

"He won't," Longarm said. "I promise you that I'll make the kid talk . . . or else."

Addie looked into his eyes and felt a shiver pass up and down her spine.

Chapter 16

It was three o'clock in the morning by the time Longarm returned to Addie's ranch and put all the horses in her barn so that they could not be seen by Wade or any of his men. Moving the horses had been the easy job, but getting the gunshot Joel Crawford moved had been a bit trickier. Longarm and Addie had hoisted the semiconscious young gunfighter into the saddle, and then Longarm had climbed up behind the man and held him erect all the way between the two ranches. Crawford hadn't regained consciousness, but he also hadn't started hemorrhaging, which was what Addie had most feared.

After a long, difficult night, Longarm tumbled into Addie's bed and slept like the dead until mid-morning. When he awoke, he was surprised to see Addie holding out a cup of coffee and smiling.

"You look happy," Longarm said, sitting up and taking the coffee. "Don't tell me there is finally a ray of sunshine coming into our lives."

"There is," Addie told him. "Young Joel is conscious. I've already fed him breakfast and he ate like a horse."

"Did he say anything?"

"He started to get out of bed, but then he felt the pain of his wounds and decided to stay put. I fed him and he thanked me. Nothing else was said between us."

"Good," Longarm told her. "I want to talk to him as soon as I've had some coffee and a chance to wake up a little. Very quickly, we'll see if Joel Crawford is smart . . . or obstinate and dumb."

"I don't think he's dumb."

"We'll find out soon enough," Longarm replied, sitting up and gulping down the coffee. "How about a refill?"

"Coming up."

Fifteen minutes later, Longarm was ready to confront Joel Crawford. The kid was pale and his head was bandaged, but he was fully alert. Longarm held a coffeepot in one hand and his cup in the other. "Good morning," he said in a cheerful greeting.

Crawford's eyes narrowed. "What the hell is good about it?"

"I'd say there's plenty of good from your point of view," Longarm told him. "After all, not many men live to see a morning after being shot with an eight-gauge scattergun. You were hit five times, so you need to consider yourself very lucky."

"Well, I don't," Crawford replied. "What happened to Casey and the others that I was riding with?"

"They're all dead and buried," Longarm told the young gunfighter. "I planted them yesterday before their bodies even had time to get cold and stiff."

Crawford shook his bandaged head in disbelief. "Are you saying that I'm the *only* one that survived?"

"That's right."

"I guess that does make me lucky, unless you intend to

send me to the gallows." Crawford's jaw muscles corded in defiance. "Marshal, if that s to be my fate, I'd rather have died with the others yesterday."

Longarm sat down in a chair near the man's bed. "Joel, I'm going to give you a chance to turn your entire life around."

"How do you know my name?" he asked with surprise.

Longarm extracted the bloodstained letter from his pocket and handed it to the young man. "Addie and I found this on your body. That's how we know that your name is Joel Crawford and you have a sweetheart who would like you to marry her before Christmas and then take her to California. Betsy sounds like a real nice girl."

Crawford stared at his letter and some of the hardness left his voice. "Betsy is a fine girl . . . way too good for the likes of me."

"She doesn't think so."

Joel looked up. "Betsy would have been better off if I'd have died with the others. I'm no good for her or any other girl."

Longarm was impressed by the young man's sincerity and said, "People can and do turn their lives around all the time. You're young and couldn't have done too many bad things yet."

Crawford's laugh was cold and cutting. "That's a joke. I stole my pa's horse, rifle, and saddle. I also stole some of his hard-earned cash, too. So how low is that to steal from your own family who never had much of anything to spare?"

"Pretty low," Longarm admitted. "But you can pay him back with interest once you put your mind to it."

The handsome young man looked away for a moment.

"Actually, I had intended to do just that with the pay I earned from Mr. Stoneman. Now that money is gone."

"There are better ways to earn money than to work as a gunman for a man as ruthless and evil as Wade," Longarm told the kid. "Have you killed anyone yet?"

"No."

Longarm drank coffee. "Come close?"

Crawford shook his head. "To be honest, yesterday I was scared almost shitless when we rode into the yard and you stepped out with that big shotgun. I wanted to rein my horse around and run like the devil had ahold of my throat."

"But you didn't."

"If I had showed a yellow streak and if things would have turned out in our favor, Stoneman would have sent men after me and they wouldn't have given up until I was shot dead."

Longarm took a swallow of coffee. "So it sounds like you're kinda stuck between a rock and a hard place."

"I won't be hanged," Crawford vowed, lifting a clenched fist. "I swear that I won't!"

"All right," Longarm told him in a calm, reasonable voice. "Let's strike a deal."

Crawford's eyes narrowed with suspicion. "What *kind* of a deal?"

"You testify against Wade Stoneman before a Cheyenne judge, and in return, I ask the judge to let you off easy. Is that simple enough?"

The wounded man studied Longarm for several moments, then said, "Maybe I don't want to testify against Mr. Stoneman. Maybe I don't even know enough about what he does to help you put a noose around his neck."

Longarm didn't believe that even for a moment. "Joel, you know that Wade is behind the killings of three city councilmen and a former mayor. Did you have anything to do with those murders?"

Crawford swallowed hard. "I told you that I never killed anyone. But I was there when two of the councilmen were killed."

"Was Stoneman there, too?"

"Yes."

Longarm smiled. "That's all you need to tell a judge."

"If I do that, I'll never live to see my twenty-first birthday."

"Oh, yes, you will," Longarm said. "Because once you've sworn that Wade was involved in murder, then I'll take care of him and you'll never have to look over your shoulder again."

Crawford shook his head with disbelief. "Marshal, no one knows better than I do that you've got balls as big as watermelons. I realize that you're a man to be feared and respected. Casey was good, but even with all of us backing him, you still beat us. But . . ."

"But what?"

"But Mr. Stoneman has other gunmen. I don't think you can take him. You couldn't be that lucky twice."

Longarm emptied his coffee cup. "You think what happened yesterday was about me getting lucky?"

"Sure. Some of it was luck."

Longarm almost laughed. "Well, kid, just in case you didn't know better, whenever you have a shotgun in your fists, you are always holding a whole lot of luck."

Crawford was forced to nod in agreement. "So you're promising me . . . what?"

"Nothing except that . . . if you testify against Wade Stoneman . . . I'll ask the judge to show you leniency."

"And that means I won't hang, but I'll be sent to prison for the rest of my life?"

"I expect you might get a year in jail at the most," Longarm said. "And if you do all that I ask, you might even get off with parole and probation. You could ride back to your Betsy, marry the girl, and go make a fresh start of it in California."

Crawford shook his head with a laugh. "Man, you really know how to spin a line of bullshit!"

"I don't bullshit when it comes to my job," Longarm told him. "And I said I couldn't guarantee anything. But if the judge in Cheyenne were to be too harsh with you, I'd take you to Denver and we'd talk to another judge. One that I know would look on you with favor."

Crawford swallowed hard. "You're serious, aren't you?"

"I'm a serious and sudden man, Joel. You ought to know that by now."

"I do and I'll do it," he said, nodding his head with conviction. "I'd be plumb crazy not to take your offer."

"Good."

Addie stepped into the room. "I couldn't help but overhear your conversation and agreement. Joel, would you like another cup of coffee or any more breakfast?"

"No, ma'am. I'm full. My head hurts something awful. Worse than the wounds in my legs and side. How'd you get the lead out of my thick skull?"

"Actually," Longarm said, "you didn't get shot there. I pistol-whipped you."

"Damn, you *are* hell on wheels, aren't you, Marshal! First you shoot five holes in me, and then you crack my head open with the butt of your gun. Yesterday, when you stepped out on the porch, you were as cool as a skunk in the moonlight. You didn't show a trace of fear."

"I do what's necessary. You and those others came to do harm to Jed Dodson and when you saw us, you meant to do us harm. Am I wrong?"

"No."

"All right," Longarm told the kid. "Addie is a doctor. She insists that we wait here a few days until you're strong enough to travel all the way down to Cheyenne."

Crawford frowned. "I think we ought to go right away. Otherwise, Mr. Stoneman will come looking for us here and you can't expect that things will turn out the same as they did yesterday."

"How many more gunfighters does he have?"

"Three or four. Casey was the best."

"Then we have nothing to worry about because I still have the shotgun. Buckshot means a burying every time."

"But it's only good at close range," Crawford countered. "What you can expect the next time is an ambush from a longer range."

"We'll make it," Longarm promised. "One way or another, I'll get you to Cheyenne."

"All right," Crawford said. "And what about giving me back my gun?"

Longarm considered this request carefully. "If I do that, will you give me your word that you won't use it on me or Addie when our backs are turned?"

"I'll give you my word."

"Fair enough," Longarm said, sticking out his hand.

Crawford shook hands with him, and the kid's grip was surprisingly strong and well calloused.

"You've been working hard all your life, haven't you," Longarm said.

"I'm the son of a sodbuster," Crawford told him. "I've never known anything but hard work."

"So when did you start to take the wrong road in life?"

"I dunno. I saw a shoot-out in our little town, and the man that won was looked upon with respect. I needed some respect, so I bought a gun and started practicing whenever I had enough money to buy ammunition. I asked the man that won the shoot-out if he'd teach me a thing or two about handling a pistol, and he did."

"So you're fast on the draw and you can hit what you aim at?"

Joel Crawford nodded. "That's true."

"Good," Longarm told him. "Because if we get jumped trying to reach Cheyenne, then I expect you to stand by Addie and me and help us in a fight."

"I will," he said. "That's a fine woman. You gonna marry her?"

Longarm smiled. "I'm not the marrying kind."

"Maybe you need to change your life the way you want me to change mine," Crawford said. "You couldn't do much better than to marry a woman like Miss Hudson."

"I know that."

Crawford touched his bandaged head. "Could be, Marshal, we both will learn a lot before we get to Cheyenne."

"Could be," Longarm said. "But I already know

enough about Wade Stoneman to know that I'll either kill him or he'll kill me the next time we meet. It'll damn sure be a corpse-and-cartridge occasion."

"I reckon that's true enough," Crawford agreed. "But if he kills you, then I'm going to have to kill him."

"Glad to hear that you see that clearly," Longarm told the kid as he got up and left the room. "Get to feeling better fast, Joel. Because the hard truth of the matter is that we don't have time on our side. There was a lot of killing done yesterday, and there's still a lot more to come."

Chapter 17

It was getting close to dark and they were planning to make a run for Cheyenne, but there was a problem . . . two problems actually.

"How long have those two men been out there watching my ranch?" Addie asked.

Longarm was standing by the front window just behind the curtains so that he couldn't be seen. "They arrived about an hour ago while you were taking a nap."

"What are we going to do now?" she asked, looking anxious.

Longarm considered the question, then said, "We'll wait and see if they ride back to Buffalo Falls and report to Wade when the sun goes down."

"And if they don't?"

"Then I'll have to pay their campsite a visit tonight."

Addie nodded with understanding. "They're Stoneman's men, right?"

"Have to be," Longarm said.

"Do you think they know about all the horses hidden in my barn?"

"I doubt it," Longarm told her. "But by now, Wade

has to know that Casey failed and most likely is dead along with the others he sent. What's important is that they don't know that young Joel Crawford is with us and still breathing."

"He's not up to making a run for it, Custis. If we have to gallop, that side wound of his will reopen and he'll likely bleed to death before we get to Cheyenne."

"I don't intend to run," Longarm told her. "Let's just sit tight and see if those two hang around tonight or ride on back to Buffalo Falls."

"It's midnight," Longarm said, checking his pocket watch. "And I don't see a campfire anywhere out there, but I have the feeling those two are still hanging around waiting and watching. Guess I'll have to go out and pay 'em a late-night visit."

"Do you want me to come along with you just in case?"

"In case I get shot?" Longarm shook his head. "I can handle this. But if something should go wrong, then you and Crawford need to strike out for Cheyenne. Get him to a judge the moment you reach town. It's the only way to stop Wade."

Addie nodded with understanding. "Are you going to take the shotgun?"

"I was thinking about it," Longarm said, picking up the shotgun and heading for the back door. "I can't imagine a better weapon to use in the dark."

Longarm exited around behind the house, and then was careful to keep Addie's big barn between himself and where he thought it was most likely that Stoneman's two lookouts were camped. The sky was dark, and he could hear the rumbling of an approaching storm. If the two men that Stoneman had sent were camping without a fire, they were going to be cold and maybe even wet after the storm arrived. It seemed likely that in order to keep up their spirits, they'd have a supply of whiskey. If so, it would make getting the drop on them that much easier.

Longarm moved silently, keeping to the low places so that he could not be silhouetted against the faint light of the moon. The wind was picking up and making enough of a noise to drown out any conversation, but Longarm had a strong feeling that the two gunmen were close.

Just ahead was a small hillock, which Longarm crept up, and then he flattened at its crown. Peeking over the top, he looked down into a swale, and there was just enough moon and starlight to identify the gunmen and their horses camped in some trees. They had a small campfire and no doubt felt that was safe, given that the hill was between themselves and Addie's ranch house.

Longarm studied the camp for several minutes, and then he began to move. It didn't take much time for him to sneak up on the lookouts. In the firelight, he could see both men hunched over the flames, looking cold and miserable in the rising wind. They appeared to be asleep, but he knew that they were not or they'd have lain down near the fire.

Standing up not fifteen yards from them, Longarm raised the big double-barreled shotgun to point at the men and said, "Evening, boys! Damn miserable camping out here tonight."

The two must have barely heard him over the moaning of the wind. One turned his head and stared with his jaw slowly dropping. He started to jump up and go for his sidearm, but Longarm yelled, "Don't do it or I'll blow you both straight to hell with this shotgun!"

159

The man wisely froze, and his friend threw up his arms and a nearly empty bottle of whiskey, yelling, "Don't shoot, Marshal! Don't kill us!"

"Both of you turn around with your hands up!"

The men did as he commanded. Longarm went up to the pair and carefully disarmed them, then stepped back and said, "Turn around slow and easy and keep those hands reaching for the stars."

They were both older than Joel Crawford, but not by many years. And their eyes were pinned on Longarm's shotgun. To Longarm's way of thinking, they looked not only cold, drunk, and miserable, but scared half-witless.

"What are you going to do with us, Marshal? We didn't do nothin' wrong out here."

"Maybe not, but you were probably sent to ambush me given the chance."

"No, sir!" the shorter of the pair protested. "We was . . . we was just lost out here lookin' for strays."

Longarm had to laugh. "You sure are a poor liar."

"Marshal, we didn't do anything," the tall, skinny man said. "And if you don't want us here, then we'll gladly ride back to town. We're out of whiskey and were thinking of doing that anyway, because there's a storm heading this way and it could even bring snow."

"Boys, I can't let you tell Stoneman what you saw out here."

The pair exchanged glances and the shorter one said, "You ain't going to kill us like you did Casey and the others, are you?"

"I'm tempted," Longarm told them. "What are your names?"

"Shorty and Ben. I'm Ben," the beanpole explained.

"I could have guessed," Longarm told them. "You boys are under arrest."

"For what!" Shorty exclaimed. "For camping out here in the hills?"

"For . . . trespassing on private property," Longarm said, knowing it sounded lame. "And I'm taking you to Cheyenne."

"Cheyenne!" Ben cried. "Why, that's a damn long ways and the weather is turning to shit! We could get caught out in the open in a damned blizzard and freeze to death long before we could get down to Cheyenne."

"Life is hard and the road is rocky and long," Longarm told them. "Get your horses and walk them down to the ranch house. We'll be leaving for Cheyenne within the hour."

Ben swore and said, "Well, in case you didn't know it, Mr. Stoneman's ranch stands in the direct line between us and Cheyenne."

"Is that a fact?"

"It *is* a fact. And in this weather——"

"Is Wade Stoneman at his ranch or is he in Buffalo Falls tonight?"

"I don't know," they both said at the same time.

"But if I had to guess, I'd say he's at his ranch," Shorty added.

"That makes things more interesting," Longarm told them. "Get your stuff and grab your horses. It's time to move out."

After Longarm removed their rifles from their saddle scabbards, the two hired guns led their horses back to the ranch house. By the time they arrived, it was starting to blow snow and the icy wind was cutting like a knife.

"We've got company," Longarm told Addie as he prodded the two sullen gunmen into her house.

"They look half-frozen," she said.

"We are," Shorty told her. "We were fixin' to high-tail it back to Buffalo Falls when the marshal jumped us. Now he says that we're going all the way down to Cheyenne in this snowstorm."

Addie looked to Longarm. "It isn't a fit night to travel," she said. "We could freeze to death if the storm turns into a full-blown blizzard."

"How far is Stoneman's ranch house from here?"

"It's only about two miles as the crow flies," Addie replied. "Why do you ask?"

"I was thinking of paying him a visit tonight, if he's at home."

"Are you crazy!"

"I hope not," Longarm replied. "But it would be the easiest thing in the world to ride right up to Wade's front door and walk into his house during this storm. Everyone will be asleep and even if he has ranch dogs, they'll be curled up somewhere out of the wind."

"But . . . but why would we want to do that?" Addie asked.

"Because," Longarm explained, "if Wade is home, I can arrest him on the spot and take him down to Cheyenne with us after this storm has passed. It'll be clean and neat. Even more important, it'll put an end to all the troubles."

Addie looked over at Ben and Shorty before she turned back to Longarm. "What about them?"

"I'm going to make them the same offer I made to Crawford. They can testify against Stoneman or they can go to the gallows."

"Is Joel still alive?" Ben asked.

"He is, and he's smart enough to see that he needs to cooperate with me in order to bring Wade Stoneman down. So the question is, are you and Shorty of the same mind?"

The pair exchanged glances; then Shorty asked, "Marshal, could you get us prison instead of a hangman's noose?"

"And not too long in prison?" Ben added.

"I'll do my best, if you cooperate and testify against Stoneman."

"Then we're with you," Ben said without hesitation. "Ain't that right, Shorty?"

"Sure thing!"

"Good," Longarm said. "Just be sure you understand that I'll kill you both if you even think about trying to get free or getting back your guns."

"You got our words on it, Marshal. We're done with Mr. Stoneman and siding with you now."

"Fair enough," Longarm said. "Let's get moving."

"I'll help Joel get ready," Addie said, turning for the bedroom. "And we'll meet you in the barn in a few minutes."

Longarm nodded in agreement. He could hear the wind howling outside, and he was sorely tempted just to lay low for the rest of the night and wait out the storm. But the possibility of catching Wade Stoneman asleep in his bed and arresting the man for murder was far too powerful to ignore.

Chapter 18

It was the longest two miles Longarm had ever ridden. By the time they approached Wade Stoneman's big log ranch house, Longarm was frozen to the bone and wondering if he was crazy to have braved this storm. The wind was blowing a gale and snow blasted them straight in their faces. Longarm felt awful about forcing Addie out into this storm, and he wondered if it would kill Joel Crawford.

"There's the barn!" Ben shouted over the roar of the wind.

They rode their horses up to the big barn door, and they were all so cold they nearly fell to their knees when they dismounted. It took three of them to pry and hold the barn doors open against the wind while they got the horses inside.

Longarm lit a match, and Ben found a lantern. Suddenly, they were bathed in faint light and could see stalls and horses. It was below freezing in the barn, but compared to what they'd suffered out on the prairie, it felt warm and cozy.

"Mr. Stoneman's horse is in that first stall," Shorty announced. "That means the boss is in the house."

"He ain't our boss no more," Ben corrected.

Addie said, "Joel is half-frozen and nearly unconscious. I need some help getting him over to that bed of hay."

"Shorty and me will help you, ma'am," Ben offered.

After they got the injured young man taken care of, Longarm had the horses placed into the few remaining empty stalls and then he checked his pocket watch. It was a quarter past four o'clock in the morning. He went over to Addie and gave her his shotgun.

"If Ben or Shorty makes any sudden moves, shoot them."

"We ain't going to go against you, Marshal!" Ben protested. "There's no need for her to keep us under gunpoint. Besides, accidents can happen."

"Sit down beside Crawford and make yourselves comfortable," Longarm told the pair. "I'm going into the house to arrest Wade. Will there be others in the house?"

"Mr. Stoneman has an old woman who lives there to cook and clean. Her name is Mrs. Boller. There's also a Chinese servant that chops wood, hauls water, and does the laundry. Other than that, Mr. Stoneman should be alone. There are hired hands sleeping in the bunkhouse, but they won't be up for another couple of hours. Maybe later, given this storm."

"How many hands?"

Ben shrugged and looked to Shorty for help, but all he got in response was a blank stare. "That's hard to say, Marshal. Some of the boys will be staying in town, so I'd guess there could be three or four sleeping in the bunkhouse. It's where Shorty and I should have been to-night."

Longarm thought about this for a moment. The most important thing would be to somehow get the drop on Wade. After that, everything else would fall into place. "Is Wade sleeping with a woman in his house?"

"Mr. Stoneman has had lots of pretty women living out here with him, but they usually caused more trouble than they were worth, so now he does his womanizing in Buffalo Falls or Cheyenne."

"Good," Longarm said, glad that he didn't have to worry about shooting a woman. "Where is Wade's bedroom?"

"It's in the back of the house," Ben said. "Go through the big front room and you'll see a hall down to the right. His bedroom is at the end of it. The Chinaman and the old lady sleep at the other far end of the ranch house. Oh, I almost forgot to tell you to watch out for Fang."

Longarm blinked. "Fang? Who or what in the hell is Fang?"

"He's some foreign breed of dog. Big, mean bastard."

"Where does the dog sleep?" Longarm asked.

"Anywhere he wants," Shorty said with a smile. "Fang pretty much rules the roost. He bit the Chinaman once so bad the man nearly lost his leg. Mrs. Boller and Mr. Stoneman are the only ones that aren't scared of him comin' up behind and taking a hunk out of their hide."

Longarm wasn't at all pleased about the guard dog, but at least he was forewarned and would not be attacked by surprise. If absolutely necessary, he would not hesitate to shoot the beast. However, hitting a fast-moving dog in poor light with a bullet was chancy at best, so he said, "Addie, I guess I'd better take that shotgun after all. You've got a six-gun."

"She won't need it," Ben promised.

"I hope I won't," Addie told him and Shorty. "But you two had better understand that I know how to use a gun and I won't hesitate to shoot you if you try to help Stoneman."

"Swear to God that we won't," Ben promised.

"That goes for me, too," Shorty told her.

Longarm believed the pair. However, he was also sure that, if he were unfortunate enough to be killed in that house, Ben and Shorty would turn against Addie as quick as a snake strikes. They were men without loyalty and would go with whoever seemed likely to win.

"Custis, be very careful," Addie warned. "Especially in respect to that vicious dog."

"I certainly will."

Longarm had all the information he needed, so he gave Addie a hug and pushed out through the barn door. If anything, the storm had intensified. It was only about a hundred feet between the barn and Stoneman's ranch house, but by the time Longarm gained the front porch, his face felt like a block of ice and his mustache had become icicles.

He didn't expect the front door to be locked and it wasn't, so Longarm eased his way inside. The front room was immense and dimly lit by candles. Longarm paused for several minutes while he rubbed his frozen hands together trying to get some circulation back into his fingers. He also gave his eyes a little time to adjust to the semidarkness, and soon he could make out a hallway leading off to the right. He picked up the shotgun and cocked both hammers, then started for it. Halfway across the front room, he heard a low, ominous growl.

Fang!

Longarm spun around just in time to see an enormous dark shadow leaping for his throat. Instinctively, he slashed at the beast with the barrel of his shotgun, and was fortunate enough to crack it across the skull. The animal fell, momentarily stunned as it crashed into a table and spilled an unlit and very ornate leaded glass lamp and shade.

Longarm froze. He was in a bad predicament. Fang wasn't going to stay down for more than a few seconds, and then Longarm had no doubt that the guard dog would renew his ferocious attack.

What was he to do now? Had the broken lamp awakened Stoneman? Longarm couldn't be sure of anything, so he charged into the rear hallway, grateful for a thick rug that silenced the pounding of his boots. When he blindly crashed into a door, Longarm found the knob, turned it, and burst into an immense bedroom faintly lit by more candles.

"Hey!" Stoneman cried, sitting up in a massive four-poster, still more asleep than awake. "What the . . ."

Longarm held the shotgun steady in his big hands. "Wade, you're under arrest!"

It took the former lawman a moment or two to collect his wits, probably because he'd been drinking heavily the evening before. But once Wade Stoneman understood what was happening, he was furious.

"Goddamn you, Custis!"

Longarm was about to say something when he heard a familiar growl. He twisted around and saw Fang launching himself from the doorway. Longarm instantly dropped and the beast flew right over the top of him and landed on Stoneman in a tangle of snarling confusion.

Before man or beast could recover, Longarm aimed just over their heads and pulled one of the shotgun's triggers. The blast was absolutely deafening, and Stoneman's fancy headboard exploded into wood splinters. Fang's ferocity was instantly replaced by terror, and the big dog dived off the bed and cowered under a bureau.

Wade Stoneman was as pale as his candle wax. His mouth worked, but could make no sound at first.

"Get up and get dressed," Longarm ordered. "And I don't have to tell you that I have one more load in this gun and I damn sure won't hesitate to use it on you."

The shotgun's explosion had completely unnerved Stoneman, and he did as Longarm ordered. He was dressed in minutes, and then Longarm herded him out into the front room.

"What are you going to do with me?" Stoneman demanded, finally regaining his composure.

"I'm taking you to Cheyenne where you'll be brought before a judge and charged with the murders of three city councilmen and a former mayor."

Wade was regaining his bluster. "Dammit, Custis, you haven't got any evidence against me!"

"I've at least three witnesses in your barn ready to testify against you. And I expect that the boys in the bunkhouse, when they see the way the tide has turned, will sing like songbirds against you in Cheyenne. Your game is lost, Wade. I'm holding all the cards now."

Stoneman licked his lips and said, "Listen, there's a lot of money involved. More money than you ever laid eyes upon, and it can be yours for the asking."

170

"I thought we both understood that I won't be bought and have no ambition," Longarm told his former mentor.

"That's true," Stoneman readily agreed. "But you're not stupid. Custis, name your price. Name it!"

"You're going to hang," Longarm told the man.

Stoneman blinked and his eyes drew down to slits. "You'll never get me to Cheyenne alive," he vowed. "For that matter, you won't even get me off this ranch. Not while this storm is on top of us, and not even when it's passed."

"We'll see about that. Outside."

Stoneman paused. "Why don't you bring your friends into my house? It's a lot warmer and more comfortable than the barn."

"Maybe so," Longarm said. "But right now the barn will do for my purposes. Now move!"

"You're a fool," Stoneman said, contempt dripping from his thin lips. "I always knew you were a fool and that I should have had my head examined for taking you under my wing back when we both wore badges."

"We all make mistakes. Now move!"

Once again they were out in the storm, and Longarm stayed close behind Wade all the way to the barn. They bulled through the big door and fell to the barn floor.

"Custis!"

"I'm fine," Longarm told Addie. "Wade isn't too happy, though."

Stoneman surveyed the gathering, his eyes stopping on Addie. "I should have known you'd be in on this."

"What choice did I have?"

"I made you and Jed Dodson fair offers for your ranches! All you had to do was say yes and none of this would have happened."

"Maybe we're like Custis," she said. "Maybe we couldn't be bought."

Stoneman started to argue the point, but then his eyes found Ben, Shorty, and Joel Crawford partially hidden back in the shadows. He visibly stiffened and his face turned red with fury. "You men worked for *me*! All three of you took my wages. You owe me some goddamn loyalty!"

Ben and Shorty took a step back, clearly intimidated, but they didn't respond. Young Crawford, however, pushed himself up from the hay he was lying on and said, "You're gonna hang, Mr. Stoneman. You're no good and now I can see that as clear as day."

"Kid, I always knew that I'd made a mistake hiring you," Stoneman hissed. "I should have run you off months ago because you don't have any guts."

Crawford wasn't intimidated. "Mr. Stoneman, I rode side by side with Casey and the other men you sent to kill the marshal. I had as much sand in my craw as any of 'em, but they're all dead now and somehow I'm alive. I didn't run in the face of the marshal's shotgun . . . so you're wrong because I had both guts and luck."

"You won't think you're so lucky when I finish with you," Stoneman warned, his voice shaking with anger. "And neither will you two!" he yelled, stabbing a forefinger at Ben and Shorty.

Longarm stepped up and said, "Shut up and sit down, Wade. Another word out of your mouth and I'll feed you the barrel of this gun and paint the barn wall with your brains."

Wade Stoneman went over to a water bucket, which he turned upside down and sat upon. His eyes roved back and forth burning with hatred. "Custis, I'm not only going to take you down, but I'm going to make you suffer before you die."

Longarm raised the shotgun and said, "Open your mouth just one more time."

Stoneman clamped his mouth shut.

For a few moments, no one said a word, and then Shorty spoke. "Marshal, what happened to Fang?"

"Fang got timid real quick when I fired a round over his head," Longarm said. "I doubt he'll ever be worth much again as a guard dog."

"What about the men in the bunkhouse?" Ben asked. "In another hour or two they'll be up, and this barn is the first place they'll come to check up on and feed the ranch horses."

"I know," Longarm said. "And when they come in here, we'll disarm them one by one."

Stoneman started to make a comment, but suddenly changed his mind when Longarm swung the shotgun in his direction.

"So what do we do now?" Addie asked.

"We wait for the ones in the bunkhouse to come to us," Longarm told her. "We just sit tight for the next hour or two."

"I hope this storm passes soon," Addie told him. "I feel like, if the sun would shine again, the world and what we still have to do would seem a whole lot easier."

"It will be," Longarm assured her. "Have faith, Addie. Everything is going to work out fine."

"I sure hope so," she said, trying to sound confident. "But a lot could still go wrong."

"You're a worrier, Addie. Worrying too much is bad for your health."

"So is what we're doing here."

Longarm smiled, and replaced the spent shotgun shell he'd fired in Stoneman's bedroom. He drew a cigar out of his pocket and lit a match with his thumbnail. The smoke tasted good and the deep cold was finally leaving the marrow of his bones. If he could have, he'd have liked to have a shot of whiskey to help speed the warming process. But Longarm figured that whiskey could wait until he had the last of Wade's gunmen disarmed and ready to sing to a judge in Cheyenne.

Chapter 19

It was impossible to tell when dawn finally arrived that cold, bitter Wyoming morning. But little by little, the storm abated and a weak sun pushed through the torn gray clouds. Longarm yawned several times, then consulted his pocket watch and announced, "It's almost six o'clock. I'd expect the bunkhouse boys will be arriving soon."

"They've already overslept," Shorty informed him. "It's freezing in that lousy drafty bunkhouse even with the potbellied stove going, and nobody wants to get up in the night to feed the damn thing."

"I did," Ben argued with unconcealed bitterness. "I was always feeding it when the rest of you lazy assholes slept in your warm bedrolls."

"Oh, shut up!" Stoneman groused, looking anxious and tired. "None of you are worth the powder to blow you to bits. Casey and I were the only ones . . ."

He stopped, realizing that he was putting a noose around his own neck with his own loose tongue. Glancing at Longarm, he said, "Casey and I were the only ones that had any balls in this outfit."

"Casey is dead and buried along with three others you sent," Longarm told him.

"How'd you do it?" Stoneman asked.

"Kill them?" Longarm stifled another yawn.

"That's right."

"That shotgun I unleashed in your bedroom is my great equalizer," Longarm told him. "And it sure played hell on your dog and fancy headboard."

"Damn you! That four-poster was imported all the way from Italy! Cost me over a thousand dollars!"

"Well," Longarm said, not even bothering to sound sympathetic, "you won't be using it anymore, so I wouldn't give it much thought."

"We'll see. We'll just see."

Longarm had been keeping a close eye on the barn doors, and now he saw them starting to be pulled open. "Addie, put your gun on Wade," he whispered, jumping to his feet and hurrying over to stand next to the big double doors. "We've finally got visitors."

Two cowboys struggled to pull open the door because of piled snow. When they had pried it open about a foot, they squeezed inside only to be grabbed and hurled to the dirt floor by Longarm. "Good morning. Don't move or I'll blow your heads off!"

The pair were in no mind to move when they saw Longarm and the size of the shotgun barrels. After disarming them, he tied them up and said, "How many more of you are there in the bunkhouse?"

"Don't tell him anything!" Wade roared.

"I'm the one with the scattergun and my finger on the triggers," he told the two men. "Who do you think you should answer to? Me, or Wade?"

176

"You," one of the men stammered. "There are two left in the bunkhouse. Art and Clem."

"If you're lying, I'll kill them and then I'll come back here and kill you," Longarm warned.

"Okay. Okay! There are three! Three men. Honest to God!"

"All right then," Longarm said, satisfied. "Addie, I'm going to collect those three in the bunkhouse. Don't let any of these so much as scratch."

"I won't."

Longarm bulled outside to stare up at the pitiful sunrise. He followed boot tracks through two feet of fresh snow, and found the three remaining men sound asleep in the bunkhouse, which was freezing cold. It didn't take long before Longarm had them tied up and standing in the barn.

"Looks like quite a crowd," Longarm said more to himself than to anyone else. "Boys, we'll make a grand procession when we all ride into Cheyenne and stop at the courthouse. I hope the marshal there has a big jail cell and food budget."

"We'll need something to eat for the trip down," Addie said. "It's going to be a cold and hard ride south."

"I expect that Mr. Stoneman has a full larder," Longarm told her. "Why don't you go to the house and see what you can find in his kitchen for our trip to Cheyenne."

Addie nodded in agreement and left the barn. Longarm said, "Ben. I'm going to cut you and Shorty some slack. I want you to saddle up enough horses to get us all down to Cheyenne."

"Yes, sir!"

"You'll never get me there," Stoneman vowed.

"We'll see," Longarm told his ex-partner. "We'll just see. And if anyone tries anything, I'll make them walk through the damn snow all the way into Cheyenne, and I don't care if they do freeze their feet and toes. Is that clearly understood?"

Everyone except Stoneman nodded.

"What about me?" Joel Crawford asked from his place on the pile of hay. "With all these wounds, I'm not sure I can ride that far."

Longarm had already given that very same question a good deal of thought. "Joel," he said, "you're the only one of the bunch we're leaving behind. You can stay at Wade's ranch house until you get strong enough to take a horse and ride away."

The wounded young man stared. "You're just gonna set me free, Marshal?"

"That's about the size of it," Longarm told him. "Go to Betsy and marry the girl. Take her to California and don't ever get crossways with the law again."

"No, sir! Thank you, Marshal!" Joel Crawford was so happy that tears of gratitude filled his eyes. "Maybe . . . maybe I'll become a marshal just like you."

"I'd not recommend it," Longarm told the kid.

Stoneman wasn't a bit touched with sentiment and growled, "I'll find you someday, Crawford. Nobody quits on me and gets off clean."

Crawford swallowed hard and Longarm said, "Pay him no mind. He'll be hanging by the neck in a few weeks."

Longarm waited for Addie to come back while Ben and Shorty saddled and bridled all the horses they'd need for the journey south.

One of the cowboys said, "Could we at least get some gloves and extra clothes, Marshal?"

"No. You're already wearing a coat."

"But it's mighty damn cold out there and it's a long ride!"

Stoneman shouted, "Quit sniveling, you sorry bastard!"

Longarm was amused to watch Wade and his men bicker. They all looked plumb fit to be tied. He kept his eye on everyone and the shotgun up and ready just in case anyone was going to try to be a hero.

When the barn door opened behind him, he didn't even turn, but asked, "Did you get all the food we'll need, Addie?"

"Drop the shotgun, Marshal, or I'll pull the trigger!"

Longarm twisted around to see a tall old woman holding a hammer-cocked six-gun to Addie's head.

"Drop it or I'll shoot!"

Longarm swore to himself. He knew that, if he dropped his gun, Wade would kill him for certain, and probably Addie and young Joel Crawford as well. And yet, he could see that the old woman wasn't bluffing. She'd kill Addie and then she'd try to kill him as well.

A losing hand, he thought with an overpowering sense of despair. *I'm suddenly holding a losing hand.*

Longarm had no choice but to drop the shotgun. He heard Wade's chilling laughter, and then the man said, "I guess you didn't know that she's my momma, did you!"

"No," Longarm answered. "And I don't think anyone else in this room knew it either. But I should have guessed a man like you would treat his own mother like poor hired help."

179

Wade bellowed with laughter and said, "Nice going, Ma."

She smiled a half-toothless grin that sent icy chills up and down Longarm's spine. "We'll get you untied and then you'd better just kill 'em right quick, son."

"I will, after I have a little fun with them."

Moments later, Wade was untied and holding the eight-gauge shotgun in his large fists. Longarm and Addie were backed up against the barn wall and unless Longarm was mistaken, they were both about to suffer and then die.

Chapter 20

Longarm glanced sideways at Addie, and then immediately wished that he hadn't. She was white with fear, and so he reached out and took her hand. He squeezed it, hoping it would give the young woman the courage to die well.

"I'll stand with you to the end," Addie whispered as she bravely lifted her chin.

"I'm afraid your end won't be long," Stoneman said a moment before he swung the butt of the shotgun and knocked Longarm up against the barn wall. Longarm tried to regain his balance, but Wade used the heavy gun's butt against him again, viciously slamming it into his stomach.

Longarm tasted bile and crumpled to his knees. The first blow had struck him in the side of the head and his head was reeling. Stoneman kicked him in the balls and Longarm pitched over onto his stomach, violently retching.

Stoneman laughed, and Longarm knew it was almost over.

"Get up!" Stoneman ordered. "Get to your goddamn feet!"

Longarm took a few fast, deep breaths, and somehow he made it to his feet. He wobbled like a drunk, and it was all he could do to focus on his enemy.

"After I'm done with the marshal, I'm taking you into my house," Stoneman told Addie with a terrible smile. "I'm going to show you that Italian bed that Custis ruined, and then I'm going to show you what I do to women in that bed."

Addie retreated along the rough barn wall, and ended up standing beside the prostrate Joel Crawford. "No," she hissed, head shaking back and forth. Eyes defiant. "You can shoot me right now, but I'm not going anywhere!"

Stoneman went for her. He grabbed Addie by the throat and started to pull her to him, but then Joel Crawford clamped a hand on his boot top and pulled with all his strength just as Addie shoved the rancher backward.

Stoneman lost his balance, dropped the shotgun, and toppled to the barn floor. Longarm lunged at the man and landed on top of him, swinging his fists like sledgehammers.

They rolled, gouging and punching. Normally, Longarm could probably have overpowered Stoneman, but given that his head was spinning and he'd just been kicked in the balls, he didn't have his normal strength, and he could feel Wade getting the better of him. Now the man was on top, and he was both heavy and extremely powerful.

Addie snatched up the fallen shotgun and pointed it at the two big men, her eyes wild with panic.

"No!" Longarm shouted, certain that she'd lost her mind and was going to shoot.

Addie realized what Longarm meant. She dropped the shotgun, grabbed a pitchfork, and raised it high overhead. Then, because Stoneman was on top and beating Longarm, she stabbed downward with the pitchfork and impaled him with four wickedly sharp tines.

The big rancher had one hand on Longarm's throat, choking him, and a fist lifted to slam downward into Longarm's exposed, bleeding face. But when the pitchfork skewered him, Stoneman arched his broad back and screamed like an animal.

Longarm rolled out from under the man, grabbed the shotgun, and fired in one smooth, instinctive movement.

And just like that, Stoneman's head was gone.

The old woman shrieked and fired at Longarm, missing. Longarm unleashed the second shot, and blew her completely off her feet and up against the barn wall. She hung there, impaled by blood, bone, and lead.

Addie and Longarm glanced at each other, and then she looked to Joel Crawford, who had found a gun.

"What's your move, kid?" Longarm asked, knowing it was all up to Crawford.

The kid's hand was shaking and he couldn't seem to stop staring at the headless man and the old woman pinned to the wall with buckshot.

"Joel?" Addie asked, her voice a trembling question.

He blinked, and then tossed the gun to Longarm, croaking, "I want to marry Betsy and take her to California. If that's still okay, Marshal."

Longarm still felt like retching, but he did manage a thin smile as he collected the gun and answered, "That's fine, Joel. Just plenty damn . . . fine."

Watch for

**LONGARM AND
LOVIN' LIZZY**

the 359th novel in the exciting LONGARM
series from Jove

Coming in October!

And don't miss

**LONGARM AND
THE VALLEY OF SKULLS**

Longarm Giant Edition 2008

Available from Jove in October!

GIANT-SIZED ADVENTURE FROM AVENGING ANGEL LONGARM.

BY TABOR EVANS

2006 Giant Edition:

LONGARM AND THE OUTLAW EMPRESS

2007 Giant Edition:

LONGARM AND THE GOLDEN EAGLE SHOOT-OUT

2008 Giant Edition:

LONGARM AND THE VALLEY OF SKULLS

penguin.com

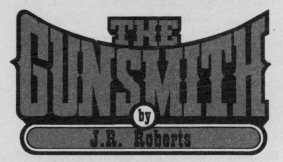